Belonging
Short Stories from Pangyrus

Contents

Note from the Editors

The short story is probably the most difficult form of fiction to bring off. You can think of it like a drop of oil, complete unto itself. No more need be said about its characters. Another way of describing it is a short work of fiction which, after you have read it, doesn't prompt you to ask, "and then what happened?" It usually, though not always, covers a short period of time, unlike a novel, which can go on for a hundred years or more. The main character in a classic story learns something or changes in a basic way between the first and last pages. The most successful short story will make the reader believe that what the writer is telling them really happened— even the most fantastical, unrealistic stories will ring true at heart. Short stories transport us in surprising ways.

The stories chosen for this anthology are some of the best of *Pangyrus*, including the three winning stories from our 2023 Fiction Contest, judged by Jennifer Haigh: first prize for *The Unbearable Weight of my Heart*, second to *We Own the Jetty* and third place to *Signs*. Each story in this anthology is unlike any of the others, a drop of oil complete unto itself, but they are united in that they all portray people in search of belonging. A drive to fit in exists just below the surface of these characters' words and deeds, a need to be seen and understood. By their family and friends, by their communities, by themselves, even by the gods.

At the core of each of these stories is a very human longing to connect. A yearning we all feel, and that is, ultimately, one of the main reasons we read and write fiction in the first place. These authors show that yearning with skill, sometimes with humor, and always with compassion. Together, these stories comprise a soulful, gritty, and entertaining collection.

As fiction editors we hope you enjoy reading these stories as much as we have enjoyed working on them and presenting them to you. It's an honor to share work this fine.

Virginia Pye and Anne Bernays, Fiction Editors
Otis Fuqua, Associate Fiction Editor

The Unbearable Weight
of My Heart

by Erin Almond

153 lbs.

Sharon, at the age of forty-three, with three kids, twelve years of marriage, and six pairs of fat pants to her name, was finally fed up. She'd been standing in front of her bedroom mirror, trying on summer clothes, when her mother called about Easter — *You're coming for dinner right, dear, with Jim and the kids? The Easter bunny has been stocking up!* — and something inside Sharon — later, she'd think of it as her "rage baby" — exploded forth. It wasn't just the way her stomach lumped over the waistband of last year's slim-fit crops, it was the tone in her mother's voice, the expectation that not only would Sharon suffer the ninety-minute drive with her family on the one day her husband didn't work, she'd also allow her children to be stuffed full of sugary treats while gorging herself on her mother's rubbery ham, a dish that Sharon had made clear she hated. As if Sharon wanted to keep getting fatter so badly it wasn't worth discriminating between shitty calories and ones — like the triple cream brie she'd had with Donna last week — that were worth the loss of self-esteem and the addition of yet another elastic waist skirt to her wardrobe.

Sharon didn't want to keep getting fatter, although she felt compelled to step on the scale each morning to track the inevitable bad news. At her highest, she'd been 192, at the end of her pregnancy with her youngest, Polly. Before that, with Gabe, she'd gotten up to 187, then eventually back down to 148, but not until she'd finished breastfeeding. (Those who said the weight "melted right off" if you nursed were, it turns out, full of shit.) Before kids, she'd been 125 pounds, always striving for

120, but creeping up to 130 during her period. Already, in her early thirties, she could no longer have a basket of fries on Tuesday and know she only had to skip breakfast until Friday to undo the damage.

Even salad was a landmine of negotiations now, since most dressings were packed with as many calories as a Big Mac, so you might as well eat that burger and fries and at least be honest about it. Not that she'd do such a thing, especially not in front of her kids, unlike her own mother who had sometimes, when Sharon's father was out of town, made a healthy dinner for Sharon and her brothers, then gone to the drive-through for her own.

Standards were different these days. No one disputed how hard it was to be a mom. Not Sharon, not her husband Jim, nor their three kids who sometimes, when Sharon was having a particularly bad day and was perhaps yelling a bit more than was actually called for, would pat her with one of their sticky paws and say, *Mom, are you okay?* Which made her feel terrible, because what was the point of all the sacrifice, the gray hair, the stretched out yoga pants, the dining room table awash in dirty socks and crumpled homework, the Legos that could never be entirely picked up so that every time she vacuumed, no matter how carefully she'd scanned the rug, she heard that inevitable crunch, what was the point of all that if she couldn't perform the most basic function of her job, that is, to be the parent, *the one in charge*, and not some helpless and somewhat pathetic person tossed this way and that by whatever happened to be howling through her life that day?

It was a sad trick of adulthood, Sharon thought, that after you'd made it through the gauntlet of middle school, and the three ring circus of high school, and the Escher-like maze of college, even after you'd beaten the odds and gotten into a prestigious graduate program in the field of your dreams, once you had kids you essentially landed back where you'd started. Now that she'd blown out her abs and could no longer fit into her professional clothing, now that she went back and forth over whether to dye her hair or just accept the inevitable, she was also in the uncomfortable position of trying to make friends with people with whom she had nothing in common other than the fact that their children adored each other. Or, hated each other, which still required frequent conversations between the parents, given that everyone had to be on high alert about bullying these days, with the suicide rates and the internet, and how much sugar and additives kids consumed, not to mention all those hormones in dairy that were giving girls boobs in third grade.

Every mom had her own way of dealing. The ones Sharon envied posted photos of their culinary masterpieces on Instagram. Or trained for marathons or fought for social justice. Sharon had considered these things, and even thought about the ways in which, back in the early eighties, her mother had dealt with the drudgery of stay-at-home motherdom. Sharon remembered cigarettes and Sloe Gin fizzes, the pungent smell of a home perm. The phone cord stretched across the living room. *Tommy wet the bed again last night! Sharon keeps climbing the dogwood, she's going to fall and break her neck! Derek thought we wouldn't find out he'd snuck a piece of chocolate cake but he forgot to wipe the frosting off his face before he hid under the table!* Sharon's mother was always talking about her children while simultaneously ignoring them, and every sentence seemed to end in an exclamation point.

By the early nineties, the cigarettes and Sloe Gin had been swapped for prayer meetings, and Sharon's mother had taken to monitoring Sharon's teenage body, making sure her jeans weren't too tight or her skirts too short, while allowing Sharon's brothers to wear whatever they pleased. When her days' work was done, she'd sit on the couch next to Sharon's father, with a giant bowl of ice cream, and watch fake families hug each other on TV.

Well, not Sharon. She wasn't going to let herself go like that. So after saying, *yes of course we'll come for Easter,* Sharon ordered a new dress, a size smaller than her current size, and vowed to fit into it by then.

Her plan was simple: no bread, pasta, rice, dessert, or wine. No meat, dairy, refined sugar, oil, or salt. She'd swap out coffee for green tea, and exercise five days a week. If this diet sounded extreme — *No wine or coffee!* Donna exclaimed at pickup, *Is that really a life worth living?* — it was only because Sharon knew that, unless she took drastic measures, she was headed for a future like her mother's, and that was the most unbearable thought of all.

***

150 lbs.

The dress arrived, courtesy of the internet and the invisible global labor that supported it. It was greenish-blue, to match Sharon's eyes, with a knee-length skirt, tight bodice, and cap sleeves that Sharon knew, no matter how much weight she lost, she couldn't pull off much longer. She waited until Polly was engrossed in a cartoon before sneaking off to her bedroom. The good news: she could get into it. The bad news: she couldn't zip it up.

Was it the right style for her, she wondered? Who could she call to ask? The biggest problem with making mom friends was that they came with more children. Take Donna, a massage therapist from Minnesota who'd moved to Boston when her husband was hired at the same Cambridge bio-tech firm where Sharon's husband worked. Donna wasn't just beautiful — she'd somehow managed to birth two kids and still retain the body of a curvy teenager — she was great fun, the kind of woman who could tile her own bathroom and polish off a bottle of discount-bin Bordeaux while she did it. Sharon hadn't laughed so much since becoming a parent, and for a while this friendship seemed like the answer to her slump.

But then there was trouble between Donna's 7-year-old son, Nate, and Sharon's 7-year-old son, Gabriel. Gabe was sweet and intelligent, but stubborn, and Nate, while also sweet and intelligent, was equally as stubborn. Often, Sharon and Donna would be in the kitchen enjoying a glass of wine — *it's five o'clock somewhere, har, har!* — when they'd hear screaming upstairs, followed by a violent smash and crying.

Growing up, if Sharon had fought with one of her brothers, a parent swooped in, assessed the situation, and spanked whichever child seemed to be in the wrong. While that was not the way Sharon wanted to parent, you had to admit there was a certain efficiency to the old methods. Now, you had to give each child their say, even last week when it had been clear that Donna's Nate was lying about the fact that Sharon's Gabriel hit him first, but Sharon knew, because Donna was right behind her, she couldn't just say *listen you little shit I can tell you're making this up*, but had to keep a concerned look on her face while he peddled his obvious fabrications. And then she had to not look *more* concerned when Gabriel told his side of the story, the obviously true side of the story, or at least the one that was easier for Sharon to believe, given Gabe's sorrowful expression but, then again, who knew? The point was that Nate couldn't handle it when someone didn't go along with what he wanted, no surprise given that his parents praised his every "insight." Yes, even wonderful Donna had her blind spots, and what did she think was going to happen when her kids grew up and got a dose of how life really was, which is to say that most people don't care about your brilliant ideas but just want you to complete the task they're paying you for, whether that's ringing up groceries or repairing a line of code.

All the while Sharon mediated this argument, she couldn't help feeling like she was auditioning for a role she was not going to get, after all. That role was Best Friend, a phrase Sharon didn't like, given its childish connotations, but here she was, back in middle school, trying to get in with one of the cool kids, and failing as badly now as she had back then.

The playdate broke up early and when a week of silence went by, Sharon wondered if maybe she wasn't ever going to see Donna again outside of pickup and drop-off. She wasn't sure if it was the boys' argument, or the way that Sharon had handled it, or if it was something else entirely, but the important thing was that her weight had gotten down to 150 that day, even though she hadn't exactly followed her diet. When Polly hadn't finished her breakfast bagel, Sharon had done it for her. When she got down to 145, she'd call Donna, and when she got down to 140 she'd get some new pants. What pants had to do with anything she wasn't sure, but somehow it seemed right to repair the relationship when she herself had reached a higher state of being, and that state clearly involved weight loss.

At 139 — what joy, at the thought of busting through that 140 pound plateau! — she might let Jim go down on her again, although it might be better to save that particular pleasure for the bigger milestone of 130, which would mean she'd finally lost all the "baby weight" and was back to her grad school weight, which was, in itself, only a stop along the way to her pre-thirties weight, her pre-Jim weight, and her college weight, all the way back to her high school weight, which at its lowest had been 105, although she understood that was probably not a healthy weight for a grown woman of her height. She'd only gotten down to it in the first place because she'd experienced a devastating heartbreak when her first love left her for a woman who was thirty-three and who, Sharon understood now that she'd reached that age and zoomed past it, really should have known better than to pick up a teenager who worked in the paint aisle. But then again who was Sharon to judge? If that mature lady had been compelling enough to make that teenage boy leave his seventeen-year-old girlfriend — who at the time weighed a mere 115 pounds — then what could she do? She could stop eating, that's what, and carve sad faces into her skin with safety pins, but only in places covered by her clothes so no one would know. And eventually she got over being dumped, and gained that weight back, although she still thought about it sometimes, how that was the skinniest she'd ever been at her adult height, and also the most miserable.

***

151 lbs.

When another week went by without hearing from Donna, Sharon wasn't sure what was more frustrating, the fact that she'd been dumped by her friend, or that she'd gone back up to 151. She tried to talk about it with Jim, but he only said, "You look beautiful to me, honey, and I've never stopped wanting you, so what's the problem?" and "If it really bothers you, maybe we should stop eating so much pizza." But, if she based her weight on whether or not her husband wanted to have sex with her, she might as well balloon right back up to 192, because her husband was a horndog who'd remained undaunted even by her 9 months pregnant self, and in fact had relished the advice from Sharon's OB to have more sex, all three times, when the babies' due dates had come and gone without any contractions, although, at that point, Sharon could only do it lying on her side, with her pregnant belly (sometimes moving when the enclosed baby shifted an arm or a leg) spreading out in front of her. The pizza comment was worse, because at least the local Italian place wasn't one of those fast food franchises Sharon's own mother had driven through when she didn't want to cook and why wouldn't Jim at least give her some credit for doing better than her own mother, instead of implying that if she weren't so fucking lazy, she might not be so fat?

"Why don't I show you how much I love your body tonight?" Jim said, when Sharon only sighed in response. "I wish you could see what I see."

"It's not how it looks," Sharon said. "It's how it feels." Still, she agreed to plan some Adult Time.

***

Adult Time

At 5:30 pm, a half hour before Jim was due home, Sharon began prepping a meal she knew, even as she was making it, that none of her children would touch and, in fact, would look at with outright disdain.

Still, she opened a bottle of sauvignon blanc and requested that Gabe clear off the dining room table and Desiree set. These requests were repeated exactly four times, while fielding questions about why wasn't Polly required to do those things ("because she's only three, and you guys didn't have to do them when you were three") why Gabe had to clear the table when most of the papers, crayons and other detritus were Desiree's ("doesn't she sometimes clear when it's mostly your stuff?"), and why Desiree had to be the one to set the table when she was the one who'd set it last night ("I'm trying to finish cooking here, can you please just do it?").

At 6 pm, Jim arrived home to eager cheers from Gabe and Desiree — Polly was amusing herself by hanging onto Sharon's legs while she moved between the kitchen island and the stove, although Sharon had repeatedly told her *mommy needs to move her own body* — and came in the kitchen to give Sharon a kiss. "Can I help with anything?" he asked.

"Maybe give Polly something to do?" Sharon nodded down at their three-year-old still wrapped around her right leg, which only made Polly cling tighter and yell, "I hate daddy!"

"That's too bad," Jim said. "Because daddy loves you!" Still, it took a good five minutes for Jim to extract Polly, and when she flung her arms around and accidentally slapped him hard in the face, Jim yelped and everyone — even the older kids — got quiet.

Finally, the tofu curry, rice and salad were on the table, along with kid-friendly foods like Cheerios, sliced apples, and leftover pasta. Polly sat down and burst into tears. Gabe reached for the apple slices and spilled his full glass of water, while Desiree sulked because she was a teenager now even though she was only ten. Sharon tried to catch Jim's eye above the chaos, but he was busy fuming over both the spilled water and the fact that Desiree had piled all the leftover pasta on her own plate, thus leaving none for the rest of the picky children.

A few minutes later, Polly wandered from the table and now Sharon and Jim could either coax her back or remind her that once she left, the meal was over, and don't expect any dessert, to which Polly would respond "what's for dessert?" and Sharon and Jim would have to decide whether to come up with something and become further irritated by having to bribe a child to, essentially, keep herself alive.

"Ice cream," Sharon said, finally. "There's ice cream for dessert."

Jim gave her a look that said he wouldn't have given in, but now that she had, there was no going back. Sharon shrugged and pulled out Polly's chair.

Polly, after finally eating some Cheerios, decided to stand on her chair and dance, although both parents pleaded "sit *down!*" Desiree and Gabe laughed so hard they almost choked, until Polly slipped and banged her head on the side of the table, and dinner ended for everyone.

"Bath time!" Jim said.

"What about dessert?" Polly's sobs dried up quick. "Mommy said there was ice cream."

Sharon avoided Jim's gaze while she poured herself another glass of wine.

Jim got Polly a tiny dish of ice cream and then ran her bath while Sharon told Desiree to clear the table, to which she responded: "But I *set* it!"

By 9 o'clock, all three kids were in bed, and Sharon and Jim took their own baths. At precisely 9:35, Jim opened the bedroom door to find a freshly scrubbed and perfumed Sharon fast asleep, snoring gently, empty wineglass on the nightstand.

***

147 lbs.

Sharon had finally discovered the secret to losing weight, which was to be so miserable that there was no longer any joy to be had from eating.

"Don't get me all worked up if you're just going to fall asleep," Jim had said the next morning. "It's not fair."

"Why didn't you wake me up?" Sharon asked, pulling a blouse over her head.

"I shouldn't have to." Jim, wearing nothing but boxers, stared at the row of shirts hanging in his closet. "If you were looking forward to being with me the way I was looking forward to being with you, you wouldn't have fallen asleep."

There was no disputing that logic, because what was she going to say — *I'll be ready to make love to you once I get below 140 pounds, make a real friend, figure out my career, and buy myself some new pants?* — so Sharon did what she always did when she had no counter-argument: she burst into tears. "At least you get to leave this house every day!"

"*Get* to?" Jim turned, his face flushed. "You mean I *get* to support our family? I *get* to come home and have my children disrespect me and my wife fall asleep instead of wanting to make love? Wow, what a lucky guy I am!"

"I would *love* to get out of this fucking house!" Sharon was livid now, too, not just at Jim's words, but at his abs, which he maintained by playing squash three times a week and eating whatever he pleased. "I'd love to spend eight hours a day in the company of adults who actually respect my ideas! What do you think I'm doing all day at home, anyway? Taking care of *everything.* You don't even mow the lawn anymore!"

"Who gives a shit about the lawn?" Jim roared. "*You're* the one who wants to keep up appearances, like some bourgeois princess!"

"Don't give me that crap," Sharon cried. "Don't try to couch your own laziness as some kind of virtue!"

"You think I'm *lazy?* You try doing what I do — you wouldn't last one day!"

Sharon, whose eyes often glazed over when Jim talked about his job, lowered her voice and backed away. "Maybe we should give each other some space."

For the next week, Jim and Sharon circled each other warily while getting coffee from the still-sputtering pot. At dinner, they spoke only to the kids. Jim stayed up late watching Youtube videos of vintage football games while Sharon went to sleep shortly after the kids. They each kept to their own sides of the bed.

All the while, Sharon fumed about how her own dad, the sole breadwinner, had taken care of the yard and home repairs and car maintenance, although there were always tasks that remained unfinished, or weren't done to Sharon's mother's satisfaction, and that had been the basis of more than one explosive argument in Sharon's own house growing up.

Where did that leave Sharon — if she didn't want to become like her own mother, who would give her father a to-do list as soon as he got home — but also wanted not to have to take care of every little thing herself? You couldn't ask without nagging, and you couldn't get help without asking, so most of the time, it seemed easiest just to do everything herself. But that shit was exhausting, and if she really thought about it, had begun to seem like a punishment for not having chosen a career that made enough money to justify paying someone else to do some of the mind-numbing tasks required to raise three kids and keep their house from crumbling to the ground.

There was no getting around the fact that Sharon had gotten an MA in Literature, which qualified her to work for almost nothing as an adjunct professor, or to make $50 a day as a substitute teacher in the local public schools. Sometimes she thought about getting certified to do something else, but the idea of going back to school and competing with childless twenty and thirty-somethings was so overwhelming she decided to wait until Polly was in kindergarten, or maybe middle school. Anyway, Sharon would figure that out once she got her confidence back, which would only take losing ten pounds, fifteen at the most.

Her stomach twisted into knots whenever she and Jim were in a fight, and this one lingered for another week. Sharon still had dinner, but she found it easy — if she allowed herself a second cup of coffee — not to eat during the day. Soon, the weight began to drop off. The secret to losing weight turned out to be: not eating. As any one of her kids might have said, *Duh!*

***

143 lbs.

The dress was still tight, but workable with the right underwear. Sharon's legs looked good when she put on strappy high heeled sandals, and she'd recently colored her hair, so someone who didn't know her might be surprised to learn she had three kids, was forty three, and hadn't made love to her husband in three weeks.

They were just packing the kids into the backseat when Donna strolled by with a bouncy brown puppy on a leash.

Desiree, Polly, and Gabe leaped out of the car — undoing twenty minutes of struggle to get them into shoes and jackets and out the door and into their seats with their seatbelts and/or car seats properly strapped. They cooed and petted the squirming puppy, before turning on their parents. "Why can't *we* have a puppy? *They* have a puppy! How come *we* never get a puppy?"

"Happy Easter!" Sharon walked over, but refused to pet the slobbering creature, even when it put its muddy paws on her new dress.

"Look at that face, have you ever seen a face that cute?" Donna grabbed the pooch's slobbering muzzle. "How can you resist?"

Sharon felt, once again, that she was being tested, and unless she gave Donna the right answer: *Yes, your new puppy is the cutest puppy in the whole history of puppies!* she would lose her last chance to be Donna's Best Friend.

But she couldn't do it — because wasn't real friendship, like any real relationship, about honesty? Otherwise, what were they doing in the end, but bullshitting each other? And that meant their friendship was bullshit, too.

Of course, there was an argument to be made that friends could be generous toward one another too, that sometimes someone just needed to be affirmed and not reminded of every little imperfection. Meanwhile, Sharon's stomach already hurt from the control-top hose, which reminded her that she was down to 143 pounds, which was great, but not quite as great as 140, when she might not have needed such uncomfortable undergarments, but what could she do but smile at Donna and compliment her puppy and try not to be pissed that her "best friend" didn't mention her new dress or that she'd dropped 10 pounds.

Which sucked, Sharon knew, really sucked, and was something she needed to think about — why she was still getting into these one-sided relationships — but she decided to table it until she *did* get down to 140 pounds, after which she'd maybe e-mail Donna telling her how much her friendship meant, but that she kind of wished Donna sometimes showed a little more interest in *her* life, so they could have a deeper, more reciprocal, relationship.

"Come on, guys," Jim called from the driver's seat, and Sharon and the kids said good-bye to Donna and her new puppy and got in the car so they could all drive to the little house on Derry Lane where Sharon had spent her childhood and adolescence, holed up in her room with the exact same feeling she had, at that very moment, pulsing in her chest.

***

"You came!" Sharon's mother greeted Sharon's family at the door as if their presence had ever been in question. She still wore her church clothes, navy slacks with a light blue sweater, a thin gold necklace with an attached crucifix lying slant across her bosom. Sharon's father had his camera out, eager to catch the kids reaching for their Easter baskets before he retreated back to his study — he had urgent work to do online, even though he was now officially retired. Sharon put her hands on her hips and grinned, hoping her new dress would be featured in one of the photos, although her father waved her aside so he could catch the real action, Polly already with chocolate smeared on her face from her hastily opened bunny.

"Guys, wait," Sharon said. "No candy until after dinner."

"Too late!" Sharon's mother laughed. Now that she stood next to Sharon's father, Sharon could see how much her parents resembled each other. Her mother had cut her gray hair short, her father had gained a few pounds, and Sharon was left with the sense that, had they wanted, they could have swapped clothes and fooled them all from behind.

Jim hugged Sharon's mom and shook hands with Sharon's dad and then looked at the three kids gorging themselves on jelly beans.

"Grandmas are supposed to spoil their grandkids!" Sharon's mother said — and what could any of them say about that? The same lax standards applied to TV watching and table manners, all of which had been closely monitored during Sharon's childhood, so that it seemed the spoiling grandmother who stood before them now couldn't possibly be the same strict mother who had once grounded Sharon for sneaking a glimpse at MTV.

And yet, of course she was, because Sharon's mother had that same face — although fleshier and more wrinkled — which wore the same expression Sharon's mother had worn for most of Sharon's childhood, one of intense, concentrated anxiety, often biting her lip, or unconsciously sticking out her tongue while breathing through her mouth in a kind of soft hyperventilation. Sometimes her expression went completely blank, before contracting with a sudden panic, the result of some internal ebb and flow of worry that Sharon's mother would never share, but which pulsed through her all the same.

"I've made ham," Sharon's mother said to Sharon. "Your favorite!"

Sharon gave her mother a weak smile and retreated to the bathroom to shuck her control top hose. An hour later, during dinner, when the two younger children wandered from the table — without having eaten a thing — Jim and Sharon caught each other's eyes and sighed in a way that seemed to indicate their argument was over, since the only way to survive the visit was for them to be on the same team.

Before the dishes were cleared, Sharon's mother brought a half-gallon of ice cream to the table, along with bowls and spoons. "Dessert time!"

Sharon bit her tongue to keep from reminding her mother of the oft-repeated rule from when she'd been a kid: *No dessert until you clean your plate!* At the same time, she decided she would have ice cream too, even though she'd already stolen a handful of candy from each child's basket (if you took from one you had to take from all). She was also wondering why she hadn't thought to bring something to change into because her Easter dress (which no one, not even Jim, had commented on, all day) was about to get even more uncomfortable.

Anyway, tomorrow was Monday, the perfect day to restart her diet, and maybe this time she'd actually stick with it, and then get back to her twenty-something weight, her high school weight, and finally even her middle school weight, because this time she was going to get it right, and make some real friends, and she wouldn't worry about whether or not they were cool, and she wouldn't have her mother standing over her, telling her what was wrong and shameful about her body (everything) and insisting that she hide herself away, and then taking up her ice cream, and her spoon, and showing how it was done.

Ask the Sea

by Khanh Ha

The train stopped at a station on the way to Saigon. The city had a new name now: Hồ Chí Minh City, named after a man much maligned among us.

I slept and then woke to the singsong voice of a girl on the train. "Cigarettes and dumplings!" She was a young teen with her hair in two plaits. She was wearing a simple floral blouse.

A few men bought cigarettes then fell back asleep. She stopped in front of me.

"How about you, *chú?*" she asked, referring to me as uncle. "Would you have a pack of cigarettes?" She handed me a Hoa Mai pack.

"I don't smoke, *cháu,*" I said, handing it back.

"How about some dumplings, chú?" She smiled. Her dimpled smile cheered me up.

"I'll take two."

She told me how much each was and I paid her. She put another wrapped dumpling in my hand. "Chú can have it. No charge."

I shook my head. "I can't take it, cháu."

"It's free, chú."

"Then how d'you make money by giving these away?"

"It's fine. My dad's tù like chú. He's not home yet."

Yes, we were reeducation prisoners. Something stabbed me and I could not speak. "What did he do before the war?"

"Mom said he taught the Viet Cong men to become better men. They used to be bad and they surrendered to us."

"He was with the Chiêu Hồi Program?" I asked, then smiled. "I know what he did."

"His name is Lê Quang Minh. Have chú ever met him?"

"Was he sent to the North?"

"Yes, chú." She counted her fingers on one hand, then laid down the tray and counted them on the other hand. "Many years now."

I simply shook my head. His bones were likely rotting in one of those stark places in the North. I said to her, "Someday he'll be back. Like me."

I lay awake. The girl had awoken a memory.

***

Yesterday was a day just like any other when we were called into the reeducation camp's meeting hall. On the podium the chief warden was reading out names of those to be released. I heard names I recognized. In that moment, I felt tremors in my hands. After fifteen years, did my hope of release ever die?

Back in my shack I sat down on my cot. Finally, I could breathe. Afraid to read what was on the piece of paper, I simply sat there. After regaining myself I peeked at the paper. I felt a sharp jab at the first words "Order of Release." I was actually being released. I breathed. The paper said my crime was being an intelligence officer of the Central Intelligence Office. I knew it was not an error. In fact, our careers under the *nguy* regime, *American enslaved puppets,* as the northern communists called us, were classified as transgression regardless.

Revived, I let myself come face to face with a fact: I was a man in his prime at thirty-five when I went to prison. My daughter was only three when I left. She was now eighteen and living in America with my wife who had left me.

Outside the shack a cold norther was blowing. This ash rain falling, falling. In my hand a blemished potato, more precious than gold. I had lost count of those fallen sick. Most would not last this stark winter. Me, a walking skeleton. Have mercy, Sir Winter. I fantasized about rice. I would bow to the ground, this gray-haired head dropped, and sing, *Hail to the holy rice.* I would chew slowly like a toothless senior masticating. But why did this stomach still feel empty?

I thought of a dear friend of mine. He died only a month back, not lasting this winter to see his release. Before he died he handed me a piece of paper. "Don't leave it out in the open," he whispered into my ear. "For you to read," he said, then tapped the side of his head. "I have it locked in here."

I hoped his parents would read this poem and know that he was a man, not a maggot:

> *They learned from chairman Mao: / Intellect is worse than a clump of feces*
> *They reform us the inmates / and we transformed feces into rice*
> *We killed our self-respect slowly / through endless hard labor*
> *until one day we lost / all our humanity*
> *In the end they have succeeded / in transforming us*
> *into what they are / the maggots.*

Outside I sat down leaning against the shack's wall. Distant stars, just dots, like in a child's eyes. Yet what I saw was simply blackness.

Of all the eyes watching the sky this night, how many naked eyes welled up with tears?

***

At sunset the train arrived at the station in Hồ Chí Minh City. My final destination. I recognized the surroundings as I stood on the platform, my knapsack on my back, watching passengers calling out to those who had been waiting for them. Had I been here before?

I shook hands with my companions and we wished each other well. One asked me where I was headed in the city. I said I didn't know and he looked at me as if I'd had a memory lapse. I said I needed some time to reacquaint myself with it. All anyone, including myself, had in his pocket was a Certificate of Interim Release to return home to live in a bigger prison. We had no identification cards, belonged to no family registers, could work only menial jobs.

Dusk fell, and I walked the streets inquiring about overnight lodging. In an alley a woman answered the door of a yellow-stuccoed dwelling. I asked for an overnight stay.

"Where's your travel pass?" she asked.

"I don't have it," I said, standing in the dimly lit doorway. "I have my release paper though."

"You were tù, weren't you?"

I nodded.

"Give it to me in case they do a house search." She scowled. "Another way to make extra money for them. Understood?"

Again I nodded.

"You pay in advance." She told me how much and I paid. "First room upstairs on the left. You're responsible for your belongings. Make sure to lock the door of your room and tuck in the mosquito netting. We have roaches and rats here."

As I mounted the stairs I heard her from behind, "Don't forget to get your release paper back from me in the morning."

Thinking of the dumpling girl again, something struck me. I turned to ask her, "Are there any buses going to Sóc Trăng during the day?"

"Two. One leaving at eleven, the other at two. Walk five blocks, turn left and go six blocks toward the river. That's where the train and bus station is."

***

The desolation of the train station had a jaundiced look in the morning sun, bronzing the tiled roof of a shack built for the stationmaster. Having heard about the prisoners' release, more than a dozen women vendors milled around, squatting on their haunches, waiting for the train. On their trays were dumplings, baguettes, and yellow bananas. Most of them only pined to glimpse a familiar face behind the train's window. A son. A husband. To know that they were still alive after all these years.

At eleven I boarded a bus. I ate the three dumplings I had bought on the train the day before. Afterward I slept. I woke and slept again, my body aching. Once I smelled a muddy odor of a river and woke and slowly gathered myself to watch the landscape of mangrove swamps lying beyond the river, and on the loamy riverbank cajeput flowers were white in brushlike bunches.

Sometime in the afternoon it rained and then stopped. The bus turned and followed a canal silty red in the afternoon sun. Along the banks were dense groves of bananas and papayas, green and dangling with fruits. The noise of the bus stirred some cormorants to wake and from deep in the groves a flock of painted stork took to the air. The bus arrived at an open-air market and the sun, now a red orb, hovered over the western horizon.

I got off the bus and asked the driver how far to the sea from the market town. An hour's walk, he said. I asked if he knew a reform camp half an hour on foot from the Hậu river. It was no longer there after 1977, he told me, then said, "Aren't you a reform tù?"

"How d'you know?"

"I know. When I was released many moons ago I was dressed just like you. Always walked around with a backpack." He offered me a light blue Bastos cigarette which I declined. In the North, most of the men — inmates and cadres — smoked Điện Biên or Vàm Cỏ cigarettes, which they disliked for their flat taste. He took a quick puff. "How long were you detained?"

"Fifteen years."

He said nothing. Then he frowned. "You must be very bad."

"Or badly reformed."

He cracked a grin. "If you want to find a place to stay, ask the woman in that café over there. If you want to unwind after all these years without a woman, ask her too."

I thanked him and left the market. The streetlights had come on when I arrived at the café. It overlooked the river; beyond the opposite bank was an island. Sampans and boats glided up and down, their lanterns hung over the bows flickered yellow and made reflections in the water. It got dark quickly after sunset. In the shrubbery of bear's breeches and threeleaf derris blinked white dots of fireflies.

I ate a bowl of caramel pork cooked with a hardboiled egg and thin slices of coconut. There were a few customers. The woman owner asked me if I was passing through and I did not know if I was. In fact, I had no place to go to. "Sis," I said to her, "I was just released from a reeducation camp."

"You have family here in Sóc Trăng?" she asked and pulled out the chair across from me. She looked in her forties and was wearing a red-and-blue polka-dotted blouse, her hair rolled up inside a headscarf.

"No, sis." I leaned back in the low-backed chair. "I used to have a family in Saigon, though."

Hearing the tone of my voice, she did not press. "I understand. I've seen many men like you. Came and left. Like migratory birds. Yeah. Those birds sometimes fall and die halfway on their journey." She watched me play with the empty bowl. "You want something else? Café sữa đá or plain black?"

"Just black, sis. What time do you close?"

"I close whenever I feel like. Usually late. Do you have a place to sleep tonight?"

"No, sis." I looked quickly over the café. It was fairly small, with barely half a dozen tables. The interior behind the eating area was dark, curtained by a square sheet of blue cloth. "Do you live here?"

She glanced back to the interior and nodded. "I'll get you coffee." As she rose to her feet she pointed toward the river where some boats had docked for the night. There were lantern lights inside their rattan domes. "Some of them rent a cot for an overnight stay. Just ask them."

She brought me a cup of black coffee with no saucer. As she cleaned the table she peered at me. "You need a companion for the evening?"

I looked at her. She smiled a friendly smile. Then after some thinking I nodded. "Drink your coffee," she said. "I'll be back."

I sat back and sipped. I could hear the sound of bamboo clapping as a boat glided downriver. It must be a vendor boat selling something at night. The breeze came in and brought a fresh smell of vegetation after the late afternoon rain. Soon the woman returned and with her was a girl in her twenties. The girl was slender. Her short hair was cut on a slant along her jawline and her oval face was tanned and fresh. She caught my gaze and smiled. I noticed her eyetooth, which made her smile all the more charming.

The woman seemed to appraise me with her gaze. "You like her?"

I nodded. The girl blinked. She was dressed in a simple collarless lemon-yellow blouse and white pantaloons. The woman gestured toward the interior behind the cloth curtain. "The room on the right," she said. "Just follow her."

I rose. "How long can I stay?"

"As long as you want," the woman said. "As long as no one else asks for her." She nodded toward the girl. "She's popular."

The room was dark. The girl pulled a cord in the center of the room and light came on from a low-wattage single naked bulb. A cot padded with a thin pallet sat low in a corner. The girl sat down. I lowered myself to sit next to her when she took my hand and put it on her belly. "Be gentle, anh."

Suddenly it hit me. I understood. "How many months?"
"Three."
"What's your name?"
"Bích Nhi."
"How old are you?"
"Twenty-four."
I glanced at her belly. "You're not married?"
"No, anh."

I did not want to ask what did not concern me.

Sometime in the evening, when I lay with her in the dark, hearing the clap-clapping bamboo of a downriver boat, I heard men's voices and the woman's voice. The girl told me it must be some local bộ đội seeking pleasure for the night. I listened and heard one man asking the woman, "Is she available tonight?" He had a northern accent that I detested, even though I was born there.

"No, she's in there with a customer."

"Get him out. I want her."

A silence. Then I heard the woman again, softer this time. "She's with a senior lieutenant. He just arrived from Hồ Chí Minh City."

"The whole night?" The northern accent had an edge in it.

"Yeah. He paid for the whole night."

They left. I lay in the dark with her head on my shoulder. She was soft and gentle and she asked me where I was headed, and I said I needed to find someone in the vicinity and described to her the area where I used to travel on foot from that nameless camp — my first camp — and how I would cut through the dunes to go across the salt flat to a commune. The girl said she knew the commune and had heard of the reform camp once there. "I was only ten."

There was something so poignant about the idea of these children living in this iniquitous society, that I couldn't sleep thinking about it. I told her I wished I could stay with her all night and she said she would ask the woman. She rose and went out and then came back and said I could. "Just pay her a little extra," the girl said as she lay down in the dark beside me. "She's closing for the night."

I must have drifted off to the sound of the rain. I could smell it, the rain-soaked earth and vegetation. The seaside air would smell like this in my first camp, perhaps more briny and moist, more acrid and thin, and the air would echo with the calls of shorebirds, and out on the sand-brown beach there would be sanderlings, and, far out on the sandbars, the high-pitched cries of willets. After a rain the air was cool and fresh.

The morning was gray, a steely gray of water and sand. In the early light one could not tell where the calm water's edge met the sand. The shallows brought skimmers from the sandbars where they had rested; the air rang with the birds' harsh sounds. *Ha-a-a-Ha-a-a!* I pictured them as migrants who had flown south through Vietnam to escape the cold in the North. I envied them, their freedom, coming and going with the seasons. Mornings when we would come through this coastal flat from that nameless camp, I could see far out in the ocean beyond the clanging buoy and imagined a ship to take me there away from shore where the bitter tang of the sea was the smell of freedom.

***

On one of those mornings in my first camp, I met a little girl selling dumplings. She would cross the beach in the early morning light on her way to the commune market, half an hour on foot away. She carried a bell and upon hearing it, I would know who was coming.

She said to me she was ten-years-old, four years older than my little daughter who was only three when I left. That morning, I gave her two *Lu Petit Beurre* biscuits I had brought with me during our excursion to the commune where we would trade the produce of our camp for meat and rice. I told her the next time I would give her a book to read, if I could lay my hands on one.

"What kind of book, chú?" she asked.

"Any book. Reading is good for a child your age."

"Books are useless," she said, pouting.

"They are not. Why would you say that?"

"The new regime said if things are not edible, they're useless."

"And you believe them?" I was not surprised. The propaganda of the North had begun its strangulation of the South in every aspect of life; schooling was no different. It was disturbing to see a girl her age who already had a sour outlook on life.

"Flowers are useless too, chú," she said, as if having read my thoughts on this topsy-turvy society. "I used to sell flowers after school. Now I'm selling dumplings."

"Your mommy made these?"

"Yes, chú. Would you buy some?"

"I don't have money."

"It's fine, chú. Tù like chú don't have anything."

I did not have to guess. She could read the initials "CT" for "Cải Tạo" on the back of our shirts that branded us as reform prisoners.

"Daddy is tù," she said, brushing her hair on her forehead. "Mommy said the regime sent him to the North. Very far away."

"What did he do before?"

"He was a soldier. He'd lost a leg during the war, but they still sent him away."

That morning she could not sell us her dumplings; we were penniless. However, one time we pooled the rare amount of money we had between us and bought the whole tray. It was more a treat for her than to us. Most of the time when we met on the beach, she would follow us to the commune. Some days she could sell the whole tray, but most of the time she would carry back the tray half empty, and her dejection would make me sad.

One afternoon as she followed us back from the commune, we rounded a dune and walked upon the faint footprints of some shorebird.

"Chú, look!" She pointed out a fox a short distance ahead of us. A red fox. I held her hand, kept her still. It took but a moment before I knew what the fox was after.

"Clever fox," I said to her, and explained in a low voice that the fox was following the footmarks to a bird's resting place. I added that if the bird had been smart, it would have walked on the wet sand and never left a print of its feet. The fox, impervious to the cries of shore birds, kept on trotting after the track, its fur ruffled by the wind that carried the clear bell note of a plover.

On those trips we had had guards escorting us to the commune and back. After one year we had gained enough trust from the camp, so that our team, all twelve of us, guarded only by two bộ đội youths, was tasked to leave camp early in the morning and carry our homegrown produce to a commune near the seaside. In the afternoon we would return, bringing back with us the provisions we often lacked such as sugar, salt, cooking oil, and, at times, rice. By mid-morning, after leaving the camp, we could smell the brine in the breeze and the ground was rough with fine bits of shells. Bent under a burlap bag stuffed with the camp's produce, each man labored in his climb to cross the dunes. I weaved my way between clumps of low-lying saw palmetto and crested the dune ridge among nodding sea oats. The long climb sucked the air out of my lungs. The salt laden breeze was warm on my face, and the sea boomed below. We took a short break, sitting on the sand, away from the waxy looking pear cactus. Some plucked the red fruits and ate them. I never tried it, though some the men said it was sweet.

The last time we were in each other's company we saw a one-legged sandpiper. The little girl stood transfixed by the bird's determination as it probed and jabbed at the water's edge, where the white foam was a sign of mollusks carried in by the waves. The wader retreated, hopping away from the swift surf only briefly before skipping again toward the water's edge. It did not have the nimble movement of the normal birds of its kind, their legs twinkling as they flitted about on the sand.

"Chú," she said, as she looked up at me, "can you make his leg normal again?"

I was surprised she did not ask, What happened to his legs? I shook my head. A pause, then, "I can't. Nobody can. I don't know what's injured him. A trap might've hurt him, or a fox might've gotten him. He might heal again, or he might not, ever."

Thinking of her, I could not help imagining the precarious lives of the sea creatures, and those of humans like hers and mine.

That afternoon we came back through the coastal flat. It dawned on me that I had not even known the little girl's name. Something told me it was the last time we would see each other, and I felt empty as if she were my own daughter about to say farewell to me for the last time. We were walking above the tide line, sometimes kicking up litter of sticks and seaweeds and shells, catching sight of crows pecking at dead crabs and sea refuse. The air was full of sounds of the stirring of wings, the sound of bird voices, of sweet pipings, and the occasional cries, like laughter, of newcome birds squeaking across the empty sky. These sounds marked the passage of time for me. Yet, for us, time was indeed measured by the sound of camp gongs, morning to dusk; for these shore creatures it was the rise and fall of tides.

Before we crossed the dune, where we parted ways, and she would get on home, going straight down the flat, I stopped and said to her, "I don't know your name."

"Hải Yến."

Her voice was innocent, and she did not look surprised when I asked for her name.

"Pretty name," I said, picturing the graceful swallow known for its tireless wings.

***

In the early morning I woke and went outside. The woman was not in the café. In the rear, Bích Nhi was washing herself by an earthen vat. The morning breeze was fresh. Her bare shoulders had a gentle slope as she bent to pour water over them. There was a scent of holy basil on the breeze. It came from the water she had boiled in a brass pan. She let me use the rest of it to wash myself. It was getting bright now and the kapok blossoms were crimson red against a blue sky. Something I had thought during the night while I dried myself came back to me.

"Is there anything around here I can do to make some extra money?" I asked her.

She wrapped herself around the shoulders with a towel. "In the marketplace, anh," she said and pointed back over her shoulder toward the river. "Plenty of boats carry stuff to the market every day. They always need a helping hand to load and unload stuff."

I thanked her. She said, "Anh can find a place to sleep at night in one of those boats." She added that it was safer to sleep there, because the local security rarely searched the boats for those who possessed no travel passes. "When does your release paper expire, anh?"

"Soon," I said. "I don't intend to go back to Hồ Chí Minh City."

The girl said goodbye and left after the woman owner returned. The woman told me which boat would take me to the seaside. By boat, she said, it would take half an hour.

As the boat pulled out she stood at the door waving. Over her the sign in red lettering said, "Pleasure Café." I was thinking of some simple, down-to-earth name to replace it, then realized I was no longer living in the traditional society which I'd left all those years ago.

Toward the sea where the river emptied itself, the turbulent water roiled red. A mist was veiling the water. Heat was rising. In the bushes along the riverbank birds were keeping themselves away from the heat. One or two would fly out, hovering over river hemp shrubs yellow as corn.

It was eight in the morning when I found my way to the seaside and saw the dunes. Years before, I would arrive here about this time and rest on a dune, and the little girl who sold dumplings would soon appear. Now I sat alone, breathing in the briny air.

Wouldn't it be a miracle to see Hải Yến, the little girl, crossing the sand flat, her bell tinkling? After all these years, was she still selling dumplings? I pictured her, an adult now, crossing the beach, a bell hung on her shoulder pole so that, upon hearing it, people would know who was coming. After a while I went down to the sandy flat when the sun was high. The green weed covering the rocks began to dry, turning the weed white and stringy, and the gulls stirred awake from their slumber and stepped gingerly along the cove's rocks, probing for crabs and snails under the crinkly heaps of weed. An acrid odor hung over the drying rocks.

I waited for a long time until the sun became too hot and I returned to the town. To save money, I walked back.

For days I loitered in the marketplace and found odd jobs that paid me a modest sum. At night I slept in a boat whose owner was a man in his fifties. He ferried farm produce from those who grew crops year round. Sometimes I helped him load up his boat from a distant farmhouse and then unload sacks of produce at the town's market. There were days I did not have time to visit the seaside, but I always thought about it. There were also days I sat on a dune with the sun in my eyes and watched the beach for the girl. She must be Bích Nhi's age now. I would listen to the sound of the bell but hear none. The boom of waves came and went, a brief lull, and I could hear the soughing pine needles in the wind.

One early morning I found myself back on the beach after the high tide. There was no sign of rock-dwellers — the barnacles, the snails — only the gulls perching on ledges of rocks above the tide mark, their shapes white, yellow bills tucked into their breasts, dozing in the sun. I sat for a long time on a dune until my shirt became dried of sweat and my eyes tired from watching the empty white sand. Then, in the breeze, came the sound of a bell.

A girl shouldering two round baskets balanced on a pole appeared around the bend of a dune. She walked quick-footed, the bell clinking.

I left the dune and went down. I stood on the shore, feeling the spray of crashing waves on my face and on the sand several crabs were washed out of their burrows and kicking in the liquefying sand.

The girl came toward me. Her bell tinkled. She wore a bright orange blouse the color of the stains on the sea-facing rocks. She lifted her gaze and I could see her face now. I recognized her.

Art Thieves

by Ann Russell

The day the Master died, I went out the back door, knowing that the party was over. My easy life as full-time electrician and handyman at the chateau was finished. Everyone on the staff knew it was the end of the line. Jacqueline, the artist's widow, was waiting to see what his illegitimate children, who had never liked her, would do next.

On the parking circle, my cousin Laurent, who worked as chauffeur, waited for me, dangling the keys to our employer's Rolls Royce. For the two years that I worked at the house, Laurent made me pretend we didn't know each other, as if he were ashamed of me.

"Shall we go for a last ride?" he asked.

I knew it wasn't right, but I nodded, and off we went through the olive groves, as darkness gathered in the tall cypress trees. The car purred over the empty road, the leather interior and rosewood steering wheel exhaling a new-car fragrance.

At last Laurent stopped the car in a secluded forest. "This is yours," he said, twisting toward the back seat where I saw five or six flat, gray cardboard boxes.

I recognized them from when I'd installed the security system in the studio. His work. I pictured the signature that would be there in the corners, the bold flourish of the P in Picasso, the twin s's like the charge of a bull. "I want you to have part of his last gift to me." He handed me one of the boxes. A gift? Was he kidding? My eyes must have expressed my confusion, because he added, "I'm leaving the region tomorrow. We can never be seen together again."

I pushed the box away, but Laurent wasn't about to give up on me. "Think of this as your retirement plan. Today you might get half a million dollars for what's in that box. But in ten years, those drawings will be worth at least forty million."

He dropped me off in back of the big house. I sat alone in my truck for half an hour, regretting the loss, in the same day, of my boss, my job, and my cousin.

***

Two years before Picasso died, my cousin Laurent, an ex-striker and local hero, called me and told me to meet him at 3:00 pm at the bar of the hotel in Antibes, not far from the town where I lived. I ordered a cup of tea so the waitress wouldn't hover. Laurent was forty minutes late. I hadn't seen him for more than a year, since he'd become the chauffeur for the Picasso family at their house a few miles inland from Mougins.

"Eh, Michel, still a wimp, I see." Laurent breezed into the room, making the table cloths flutter like women's skirts. Laughing and boasting about his winning bet on the World Cup soccer match in Brazil, he kissed me on both cheeks. He had shoulders like a bull, a rugged but handsome face. He ordered a pastis and gave my tea cup a pitying look. "You're almost thirty. Time for you to grow up."

Laurent, ten years older than me, had taken me under his wing when my father died. I was twelve at the time, a gangling adolescent, always out of focus in my school photos. He helped me with my homework, explaining the hard stuff like negative numbers or the plays of Molière. He brought me to watch his soccer matches.

Once when two older boys tried to grab my lunch on my way to school, Laurent came cruising by in the taxi that he drove back then. "Don't mess with Michel," he roared, jumping out and punching the bigger kid. As I grew older, he encouraged me to become an electrician like my father.

Laurent's pastis glass looked fragile in his powerful hand. "You know who Picasso is, right," he said. Everyone in my village knew that a famous Spanish artist lived in the next town and made ugly paintings of nude women. "Today's your lucky day. Picasso's wife Jacqueline wants to hire an electrician." He handed me a note with a phone number on it. "Call her and tell her you're interested. You know about installing security systems, don't you?"

I'd been putting in perimeter alarms and motion detectors for my rich summer clients. But these jobs kept me employed only in the season.

"It's a big job. If she likes your work, she'll keep you on as a full-time handyman. Big chateaux always need an oven repaired or old wiring replaced."

Proud that Laurent would recommend me, I felt my troubles lifting.

"You mean I'll be working in the same place as you? I'll get to see you now and then?"

"Not quite. There's one small matter," he said. "You can't let on that we know each other."

"Why not?"

He ordered another pastis and glanced around the room. "This job is a big step for me. I'm meeting a lot of important people. I can't afford to lose my credibility with the Picassos if you screw up."

I felt taken aback that Laurent didn't want to associate with me. But I was delighted at the prospect of finding year-round employment. Finally, I could marry Sabine, the prettiest girl in my neighborhood, before she married some other admirer.

***

When I started working at the house, Picasso was ninety years old and wheelchair-bound. Only Laurent could move him from his wheelchair to his leather armchair. They spent hours together watching soccer on TV or playing dominoes. I overheard Picasso telling him about his early years in Paris, his opinions of other modern artists who'd been in his circle. It felt odd pretending not to know Laurent. But Jacqueline was always kind to me, giving me fresh croissants in the kitchen and asking me how my new wife Sabine and I were getting along.

When I'd married Sabine, a few months after I began my job with the Picassos, there wasn't even running water at my house. She had to use the rusty pump to wash the dishes. In our year together, I'd put in a connection to town water and bought new appliances for the kitchen. Every night she made wonderful dinners for us. We were happy together.

"I wish you'd look in on Pablo," Jacqueline said to me one morning a few months before the artist died. "Laurent's gone out. Maybe you can keep the old man company."

When I stepped into the master's day room, he was alone, sitting in his wheelchair. I couldn't tell if he recognized me. I readjusted the thermostat, so he'd know I was on the staff. He looked up and started murmuring to himself. His head was as round and smooth as a bowling ball, his eyes dark and unreadable. The stitches of his fisherman's sweater stretched across his ample chest.

The room was filled with canvases stacked upright against the bookcases. A wooden mask with a bulging forehead hung on the wall behind his desk. Its small round mouth reminded me of a funnel. Next to the window was a drawing of a bull-man, I once heard Laurent call it a minotaur, towering over a nude model asleep on the floor of an artist's studio.

After a while, the master emerged from his daydreams and said in a papery voice, "I was your age once, young man. I lived in Paris. Women used to fight over me. Now no one fights over me but my family."

Here I was, alone with Picasso, the most famous artist alive, according to the cook. Perhaps he'd like to play cards, I thought. I looked down at the dirt under my fingernails and was too embarrassed to suggest it. I asked if he wanted to sit by the window, and he nodded. I rolled the chair across the room and lifted his old legs onto a foot stool, surprised to feel how thin they were. I tucked him in with a blanket, the way I'd seen Laurent do when the two of them were playing dominoes and smoking cigars.

"Where's Laurent?" His white eyebrows furrowed.

"Nobody's seen him this morning. Marie says she doesn't know where he is." Marie, Laurent's wife, was Jacqueline's long-time chambermaid. They lived in the back wing of the house. I could always hear Marie approaching, because she carried a ring of keys, even bigger now that I'd installed the security system and turned over the keys to her. In recent months, Laurent occasionally disappeared for hours at a time while Picasso was napping.

Picasso looked lost. Laurent was his only friend in this big, lonely place. Soon the master fell asleep. I couldn't tell if he knew who I was or not. I was afraid he'd wake up and think I was an intruder, ask me what I was doing here, or worse, what I thought about his paintings. The cook once told me that his initials and a squiggle or two on a piece of paper was better than currency.

***

The night after Picasso died, I pulled my truck up my unpaved driveway. Without daring to look inside, I hid the box Laurent had given me in the shed next to the rustic house I had built. When Sabine told me, a few months ago, that she thought she was pregnant, I'd promised to build an extension on the house for a second bedroom. We'd sat around for hours thinking of names. The night after Picasso died, she told me she'd been to her doctor, who'd confirmed that the baby was a boy.

Now I had to worry that the boy's future could be ruined if anyone discovered the box in my shed. All through dinner, I felt disturbed and anxious about the box. After Sabine fell asleep, I crept out across the driveway. The moon was shining through breaks in the ragged clouds. I lifted the lid off the box, and a drawing of a woman caught my eye. It was sketched with a few heavy blue lines on cream-colored paper.

At the sight of her, an electric current ran from my eyes to my gut. Her body looked like it had been cobbled together with parts from a baboon and an old-fashioned coffee percolator. Her narrow face was elongated by a chin that resembled the heel of a miner's boot. Her large, pointed nose was folded over to one side. A thinner line, from the inside of her hip, trailed down to the tiny blue bird's nest between her legs.

"Hideous," I said aloud and pressed the lid down on the box. Who would pay tens of thousands of dollars for such a drawing? I thought of tearing it up, but I couldn't quite bring myself to do it because Picasso had been decent to me during those last months of his life. I felt a wave of nausea and swore never to look inside the box again. I had become not its guardian but its hostage. As I tried to sleep that night, I was pursued by visions of women with noses like dog snouts, and bulls with burning red eyes.

"What's wrong with you?" Sabine asked me the next morning, stroking my hand.

"Nothing," I said, unable to look at her. I didn't want to find myself thinking about the animal-woman who'd taken up residence in my shed and my brain. That night I returned to the shed and shoved the box onto the highest shelf. It sat there for four decades.

***

I didn't notice the sputtering of a missing cylinder in my engine until I turned my pickup truck into the driveway that, according to my directions, led to my cousin Laurent's house in Languedoc. I pulled into the parking area, surrounded by a manicured lawn edged with roses, and let the engine shudder to a halt across from the front door. The buzzing of the cicadas punctuated the ensuing silence. At the sight of Laurent's imposing residence, my vision of a cheerful reunion faded. I felt like I was visiting a rich client, not a family member who used to carry me around on his shoulders when I was a boy. Already I had second thoughts about my Sunday afternoon visit to a man I hadn't seen or talked to for a decade and a half.

Recently, I'd read in Le Monde that he was having an exhibition of his collection of Picasso drawings at a gallery in Paris. There were photos of him arm in arm with artists, writers, and politicians, just like I'd seen him at dinner parties at Picasso's house. Times had been harder than usual for me that year. It had been a cold summer in the south of France. The hotels I now worked for were less than half full, and they weren't spending money on renovations or repairs.

I remembered the evening we'd left the big house, when Laurent told me we couldn't be seen together again. When I looked hurt, he'd said, "Three people can keep a secret, but only if two of them are dead." But fifteen years had gone by, and I hoped he might give me a helping hand.

"Nice gardens you got here," I called out to Laurent, who was pruning the boxwoods. The stone house with its floor-to-ceiling windows looked like a smaller version of Picasso's house. I knew Laurent would remind me that he'd given me a whole box of Picasso drawings, which ought to make me richer than most of my clients. But since I knew nothing about the art market, I had no idea how to sell drawings that I strongly suspected to be stolen. It took someone bold, like Laurent, to do that.

"Whoa," he said, gesturing to me to back off as I got out of my truck and came toward him with open arms.

"Aunt Berthe gave me your address," I said. "I went to visit her last winter." Laurent had gained a lot of weight and had gray seeding through his once dark hair. "I've come all this way to talk with you about old times."

"What times were those?" he asked.

"Don't you want to know about how I'm doing these days?"

"I think I can guess." He slapped a cricket that landed on his forearm.

"No. You can't guess. I have two wonderful sons. Smart. They plan to become engineers. You should meet them."

"I'd like to. Believe me, I would. I'll keep them in mind and try to do something for them."

Looking all around to make sure no one was listening, I took a step closer and confessed, "I'd like your help with selling my art works."

"As if I didn't know that. Poor Michel. I hoped you might at least have had a little talk with a local art dealer about how to go about selling a souvenir or two from your former employer." He gave a sour laugh. "Go home. If it gets around that you're my cousin, and that we both worked for the Picassos without their knowing it, the game's over. For both of us." I'd come all this way to ask his help in selling my drawings, but he had no support to offer me.

"Couldn't we just talk? Like about Aunt Bertha. She's in a nursing home now, you know."

"I've talked with her. Who do you think is paying her bills?"

"I never should have agreed to take the box. Not even for a million dollars' worth of art."

"A million? You're behind the times. Try forty million in today's art market." He sniffed. "I told you to hang onto them. Who else ever gave you such good financial advice, eh? You disappoint me, Michel. You just don't get why we need to stay apart."

"I don't know anything about selling art. You could tell me what to do," I said.

He raised his massive shoulders like one of Picasso's minotaurs. "Find an art dealer in the region and sell them one at a time to avoid raising suspicion."

"The problem is, I don't want them in my garage." I scratched behind my ear. "I live in constant fear they'll be discovered." I paused as if waiting for him to spare me from what I was about to propose. The cicadas sang in a single mighty voice, and white tufted seeds swirled down like tiny parachutes. "Look, I'll give them to you. If you sell any of them, you can give me a little commission." If I had a choice, I would rather have my cousin back, the way it used to be, than the drawings.

Laurent laughed at my clumsiness. "Sorry, I can't help you. I have too many drawings of my own to sell. Besides, if I took the drawings off your hands, you could rat me out at any time."

My neck snapped with surprise. Did he really think I would do that? I laughed as if he were joking, but it was clear enough he didn't trust me.

"How do you do it?" I shifted the weight on my feet. "Selling your drawings, I mean?"

"Picasso's daughters adored me. When they visited the house, they nicknamed me 'Teddy Bear' and wanted to ride around on my shoulders. They were the ones who sponsored the exhibition of my drawings in Paris last year. Now I'm legit. I can sell my drawings openly, and I can afford whatever I want." He paused. "Except being related to you."

Laurent made a move toward his front steps, and for a moment, I thought he was going to go inside and ignore me. His wife Marie, who had worked as housekeeper, appeared at the door. She was the one I'd taught to operate the alarm system in Picasso's studio. Of course. That's how Laurent pulled it off. How had I failed to put the pieces together before?

"Who are you talking to?" she asked Laurent, her voice like a dentist's drill.

"No one, *chèrie*." He scowled as he glanced toward me. Behind the screen door, I saw she held back a German Shepherd by its collar.

"Then it's time for him to leave."

Laurent turned up his hands as if to indicate he was powerless to oppose his spouse's wish. I turned toward my truck and felt as if a metal door had slammed shut behind me. I dragged myself across the driveway and sank into the driver's seat of my truck. The engine rumbled to life. It was a long drive back to the Côte d'Azur. The darkening highway taunted me with my helplessness. My sons deserved a better father.

***

Many years later, I was on one of those high-speed trains to Paris for the first time in my life, barreling through the lavender fields of Provence at 250 kilometers an hour and past hillsides dotted with poppies like scarlet coin purses. I'd retired a few years ago with a modest government pension after being diagnosed with cancer. Sabine made sure I took my medications and grew vegetables in our garden.

My sons had become engineers and had high-paying jobs now. Last summer, they brought their families to the South of France to visit Sabine and me. We took our grand-children to a local soccer match, and they made fun of our regional accents.

One day when I was out in the garden planting tomatoes, Sabine brought me a cup of tea and asked me what would happen to her after I was gone. That was when I knew I needed to do something about the box of drawings that had sat untouched in my crumbling shed all this time. Someone might stumble across it, and she'd be dragged into a criminal investigation.

I'd prepared my story long ago in case the box was ever discovered: Jacqueline Picasso handed it to me the day the artist died. By now I could almost remember the conversation, the two of us standing in the drafty hallway next to the vaulted kitchen. Jaqueline herself had died decades ago, at which point, Picasso's three illegitimate children had gained title to all of their father's unsold art works. Laurent died the year after Jacqueline, and his wife retreated to their house and lived as a recluse until she died a year ago. There was comfort in knowing that everyone who could contradict my story was now dead.

At a street market in Cannes, I talked with a couple of dealers who sold cheap reproductions of Picasso prints about how to sell Picasso drawings. They told me I needed to have them authenticated by the Picasso Foundation in Paris, established by his three children after they took possession of his estate.

***

The *hotel particulier* that housed the Picasso Foundation was just off the Place de la Concorde in Paris. The chrome and leather chair I sat in was uncomfortable and squeaked when I shifted my weight. The Foundation's administrator, with whom I had made an appointment, bustled into his office thirty minutes late.

"So, you were the electrician," he said, sliding his glasses down his nose with one finger. "Are the drawings in there?" He pointed to the faded box. "Could you put that on my desk, please?"

He appeared to be in his mid-sixties, several years younger than me. He leafed through the first twenty drawings, one at a time, stacking them on his desk with care. He studied a few of the sheets at length and muttered, "I see. I see." My stomach heaved. What did he see?

He started to flip through them more rapidly, ten or twenty at a time. "The unusual thing about these drawings," he said, "is that they're unsigned. When Picasso gave a work of art to a friend, he usually signed and dated it, knowing that the individual would sell it."

"Jacqueline gave them to me," I hastened to say.

"A number of these works appear to be early ones, from his Cubist period."

"I'm no art expert," I replied.

His smirk said he was aware of that. "The numbers on the backs of these drawings match up with the complex numbering system Picasso used throughout his life. They're definitely authentic."

Numbers? What numbers? I'd never even looked at the backs.

"I have just one question for you." He tented his fingers. "Why would Picasso give so many drawings to you?"

"I was Jacqueline's friend. She's the one who gave them to me."

"Yes, but more than two hundred original art works? When you made the appointment, I imagined you might have two or three." He flipped through them again and pulled something from the bottom of the pile that looked like yellow paper, typed with numerous overstrikes. "What can you tell me about this?" he asked as he studied the pages.

The writing on the paper appeared to be a list. My mind spun in disarray. I never even knew these yellow pages were there. Had Laurent made a list of the contents of the box sometime before he gave it to me? Not knowing what explanation to give, I said, "I made it."

"It appears to be an inventory. Here's an intriguing entry, 'Strong resemblance to a Cubist harlequin drawing in the collection of MoMA.'" He gave me a little sneer. "What does MoMA mean to you?"

I didn't know what he was talking about. "I don't remember," I said. "My local librarian helped me make the list. She looked up a lot of information." For good measure I added, "She's been dead for ten years."

"I'll give you a clue. It's in New York." He scratched his throat under his tie. "The thing that intrigues me is that, just a few weeks ago, the French art police notified me about a group of Picasso drawings coming up for sale at an auction house in Paris, from the joint estate of Marie Reynaud, Picasso's housekeeper, and her husband Laurent Reynaud, his chauffeur. And it seems that you were named in the will as one of the couple's heirs. An interesting coincidence, don't you think?" He coughed and continued, "Of course I'm working with the police to stop the sale from going forward. When Jacqueline's estate was settled, the court ruled that all of Picasso's work that hadn't been legitimately sold or given away belonged to the Foundation."

I knew about the will and the auction. I didn't know there might be complications. When the lawyer for the estate had contacted me a few months ago to get my consent for the auction, he mentioned that Laurent had intended the legacy for my two sons. But he warned me that they didn't have that much to gain. Laurent had sold the most valuable drawings long ago, and Marie turned out to have a lot of relations who had all been given shares of the estate. But I had been excited to see articles about the upcoming sale in the newspapers.

Now here I was, wishing I hadn't been related to Laurent or that no one in the world knew we were cousins. Finally, I understood why, all those years ago, Laurent had kept me at a distance. In the end, as it turned out, it was Laurent who ratted me out, by leaving me a legacy.

As I got up to leave the office, to my surprise, the director handed

the box back to me. He glanced at his watch and said, "The Foundation
will need to inventory and certify your drawings and add them to our data
base of Picasso's complete works. We can send someone to the Côte d'Azur
to pick them up. Or we can bring you back to Paris with the drawings, if
you prefer." His willingness to let the drawings go suggested how much he
trusted the police to intervene.

"I need to get to the station now," I said, my head pounding.
"There's only one train back to the Côte d'Azur this evening."

He handed me his card. "You'll be hearing from us soon," he said, in
a way that made me not want to hear from him ever again.

Outside on the busy sidewalk, no one showed any more interest in
my old, tattered box than if it held dirty shirts.

***

Returning to my region late that evening, tired and shaken, I stopped
on my way home at the hotel cafe in Antibes where I'd made the devil's
bargain with Laurent all those years ago. The cafe looked different, no
tablecloths, an extra wide flatscreen TV behind the bar.

I collapsed into a chair in a dark corner and wondered what I
would tell Sabine, how I could even face her. Why hadn't I turned over
the drawings to the authorities long ago? I had no answers. How long
before the police showed up at my door? Laurent had played me for a sap
right here in this café, and it had taken me four decades to figure out how
calculating he had been.

"What'll it be tonight?" asked the waitress, tattoos spilling down
her arms from under her T-shirt sleeves.

"Any suggestion?"

"A pastis. Isn't that what you usually have?"

Evidently, she was confusing me with someone else. A regular,
perhaps, some sad old guy. I stared at my pastis without drinking it,
dropped a few coins, and left with the gray box under my arm. Outside the
night was dark. The clouds blotted out the stars.

Feelings

by Pamela Painter

My roommate is a zombie freak. A theatre major, she's taking the course on body craft that teaches zombie moves. Her favorite movies are *I Walked with a Zombie* and *Dawn of the Living Dead*.

I sit on my bed, sketchbook on my knees, and draw her practicing how to stumble and lurch. When I giggle, she says it isn't funny, that Hollywood always needs actors who do zombies well. She says, "It's not all make-up, blood and gore." She stops mid-lurch and glowers at me. "Maybe I'm a zombie," she says.

I laugh and point to her posters of Adele, The Kinks, and Taylor Swift. I tell her zombies are nothing like us. They don't read or write, and they can't even walk straight. "We're not supposed to walk straight," she says, lurching over to our closet, turning, and lurching back. Her arms dangle down, loose as a noose. As I sketch her straggly hair, she informs me that next fall her costume and makeup class is doing two weeks on zombies.

When she learns I applied for a new roommate for sophomore year, her feelings are hurt. I try to make a joke of it. "Zombies don't have feelings," I say. Her eyes narrow, go dead. She says, "So now you're the one out for blood." And then she laughs.

Kissy

by Pamela Painter

Kissy-I-love-her-name and I are at the local grocery, shoplifting stuff for the dorm party to celebrate getting the RA kicked off our floor. We ratted about her weed habit and her biker boyfriend crashing in her room every weekend, though we couldn't care less.

Kissy-I-love-her-name is in the next aisle over. We meet at the back of the store, giggle, and flash each other the pockets of our oversized thrift-store trench coats. I have beef jerky, crackers and two cans of spray-on cheddar cheese. Kissy-I-love-her-name has crackers and chips and also tampons, zit cream and shampoo I don't question. She's good at this activity because these items aren't covered by her scholarship. She makes me cut her hair to save money. Her dad's been laid off forever because he's a mean drunk, and her mom left home the very same day Kissy left for college and postcards never come with money.

Kissy-I-love-her-name says the liquor store will be more of a challenge. Fake IDs don't pay for booze. Our floor pooled our money. We have enough to buy two bottles of cheap gin. Kissy-I-love-her name uses her hand inside her pocket to lift two handles of gin and carefully amble out of the store. I hoist the gin, surprised at its weight. She's been my shoplifting prof for the past year. I hope there are other things she'll teach me. Kissy. I love her name.

Manifest Your Dreams

by Marie Myung-Ok Lee

The Antonio's Demolition truck slowed, then stopped at the T junction where Melody was waiting to make a left. The *thick-tunk thick-tunk* of the turn signal reverberated dully in her brain. She was just trying to get to freaking Whole Foods and back before her shift at the hotel.

She thought he was going to turn, but instead the driver made eye contact, and waved.

It took her a second: he was creating a space for her. Running interference.

After you. There was a little bit of *little girl!* in the finger flourish at the end. Cars were shoaling behind her. One beeped.

After YOU! the Demolition man's entire arm reiterated. His eyes impatient.

A sustained beeeeeeeeep. The man behind her was gesticulating, his mouth a cavernous, mutating O in the rearview mirror.

After you!

A *waagah-wagaah* horn blast from behind, the sound propelling her forward.

Where was that shattering noise coming from?

Everything, white.

Her last thought was about Caleb.

***

The white light of the afterlife was a little grayed, puckered on the edges. Figured — she was getting the Dollar Store version, probably because she was a lapsed Lutheran. She saw no relatives, or Snoopy who'd been run over as a pup, no angelic voices calling "Melody!" Then the airbag

51

deflated like an old breast, revealing a fireman peering into the car with an expression of concern and bafflement.

A small crowd had gathered along the sides of the street, flashing lights from some first responder, her car at an angle, sighing gently. A man outside his own blotational SUV, gesticulating wildly, familiar: "Of course I didn't see her!" The door to her Honda swung open just fine, smooth as ever. She emerged from the car, refusing the fireman's gloved hand.

***

"Is this Mrs. Martin?" The insurance adjuster called her the next day, just as Melody was rolling her hair into the fat sausages of her no-heat curlers, getting ready for work.

"This is Melody," she said. She was married, yes, but why did the "Mrs." thing make her feel like someone else?

This insurance adjuster guy whose name she didn't catch also made her feel like someone else — like some crazy lady driver who pulls out into traffic and basically crashes her own car and now wants money for it. Practically insurance fraud according to him!

"The guy in the truck motioned for me to go," she repeated calmly. She tried to describe the accident, and how she proceeded, the guy had barrelled out of nowhere. Luckily, because of some excellent safety reflex, she'd turned the wheel toward the curb, and he'd just clipped her car in the corner instead of T-boning her. It could have been way worse! And how soon could they fix it? She could hear her own voice, how young and feminine it sounded; she was aware of her vocal "fry." She did it unconsciously because it felt good for her voice to catch on something, like gears, instead of just floating. As she held the phone in her hand, bouncing gently on the bed, she stared out the window at her Honda looking oddly pristine at the curb, as all the damage was on the other side.

"The witness said you pulled out without looking."

"The driver in the Antonio's Demolition truck *told* me to go!" She rolled her eyes, canted her head toward Caleb, puttering in the bedroom, not looking at her, and clearly, not listening, totally missed his cue.

"*He* told me to go," she repeated, a little louder, both for the adjuster and for Caleb. "He could see the oncoming traffic and I couldn't." Hello: *To double-check would have been to question his authority.* They should give women drivers women insurance adjusters. Navigating men and their fragile feelings was what women had to do every day. Anyone remember that woman on the internet who laughed at the guy who catcalled her, and he shot her?

AMCAR Insurance, he said, would allocate $500 for the repair, that's it. She pointed out that there was something wrong with the engine because she'd had to have the car towed, and $500 wouldn't take care of it. He mansplained back she was lucky the guy that hit her was in a huge SUV and had suffered minimal damage. Putting in more money than that would be "betterment." which wasn't covered.

"What about pain and suffering?"

"He's letting you off the hook this time."

"No, I mean for *me*." The last time she'd gotten into an accident (rearend, young dude rushing from happy hour to return his Zipcar, back when she and Caleb were in college), the whiplash had taken a whole two days to show up.

He snorted. "Are you for real?"

***

No sooner had she hung up than she spied first what she thought was an unseasonable leaf flown under the wiper but then saw it was a ticket — probably for parking on the street overnight. Last night, the tow truck driver had pulled up to the house with a "This good, sweetheart?" At the time, too mentally exhausted to instruct the driver how to place the car in the driveway at the precise angle to not obstruct Caleb's car in the garage without sounding like some entitled little blond girl, she just said "thank you, that's great." Ugh, why hadn't she had the car towed to the shop and had Caleb come get her? But again, embarrassed. Worried about Caleb's reaction.

She ran out in her big T and leggings, across the short lawn, the curlers in her hair swaying like cattails, and snatched up the ticket. The grass felt cool under her feet, but she worried momentarily about pesticides. This was the yin/yang over her life, a low-level feeling of everything she did being wrong. Like whatever was the opposite of "slay." How was she going to get the car to the repair place when she'd used up the one tow that came with her AAA instinctively just to come home.

Caleb, she hoped, would give her a ride to work. His schedule was flexible. Hers was not. He was still getting ready, so if she hurried, they could leave together. She dressed, added earrings, shrugged on her suit jacket, slipped on her regulation 1.75" heels. The sky was brilliant, almost mockingly clear — what a waste to spend the whole day in the lightless lobby of the Arcade Hotel.

"Babe — you leaving for work soon?" she said. Any female friend would immediately reply, "Yes — oh, do you need a ride, since your car is out of commission?"

"Yep," Caleb said

She murmured that it would be nice to get a ride. She kind of said it like she was saying it to herself. Because she didn't want to be disappointed. She impaled the lapel of her jacket with the pin that said *Melody/Guest Associate.*

He had his chin in his hand. Sometimes, he had experiments he had to get to at certain times, maybe he was too busy.

But also, there was a podcast running on his laptop.

Next up on Show Me the Money: The new Cayman Islands? The friendly legal and accounting climate in the Turks and Caicos, including no extradition treaties, have caused this place to be almost overrun by WEIRDs — Western Educated International Rogues & Dictators....

She noticed a pain, radiating into her temples. Not worth

complaining about, but should she say something, in case it got worse? Wasn't there that actress who only fell lightly on a ski slope (she laughed about it, Melody recalled) but later had a brain bleed and died that night in the hotel? Can one get a concussion from being punched in the face by an airbag? She indeed had the lavender suggestions of two black eyes. She didn't want to go to work. But she didn't have a good enough reason not to, especially since she had to cancel on Jose last night, and rumor had it the next assistant general manager might be an internal candidate.

"I guess I'll have to call an Uber." She left that one hanging. He didn't respond.

Time to slay, time to slay, she murmured to herself. She was an independent woman. She could get herself to work. The curlers had worked great today, her hair fell into soft waves that framed her face—but she resolutely started combing it out. A bun would be more managerial. Plus, thanks to a salon treatment she'd splurged on, when she smoothed it close to her head, it shined like a trophy. She reached for the Costco bottle of generic ibuprofen and tossed it in her bag.

***

The next day, her headache had not abated. In fact it might have been slightly worse. Her neck, stiff. Googling her symptoms led to the same conclusion: SEE YOUR DOCTOR IMMEDIATELY. If it turned out she had a brain bleed and died, would that change her insurance payout? she couldn't help wondering. She hadn't mentioned the pain to Caleb yet. He had a conference this week and looked so constantly stressed preparing for it, there never was a good time.

She was always a little jealous when he strode off with his hardsided wheelie bag that looked like a Lego. He was out doing stuff, "career development." She didn't have a suitcase like that because, despite being in the "travel industry," she basically didn't travel. Neither of them made much money right now. He was a post-doc who worked in a lab that

studied mono layers, meniscus, lateral flow states (whatever that was) —
stuff that had "industry applications."

She had to admit she was envious of the well-defined steps of
Caleb's path. MA. PhD, post-doc. Her future was a vague hope for more
money, a more interesting life, how about a promotion (but did she really
want to be an Assistant General Manager, i.e., harried Jose?). Scanning
the Instas of her college friends, she saw many had jobs that sounded
important. *Commodities trader. Content creator. Branding specialist.* The biggest
slacker in her college marketing class, Seth Dimas, was already a CEO of
some rideshare scooter startup. How does that happen? Time brought
more interesting things for some people. For her it felt like it was merely
running out, sand through a glass. She was a young(ish), pretty woman,
definitely above average in looks (as her mother and grandmother had
shown, always fussing over what she ate, what her hair looked like, fretting
over the blond darkening when she was five), but was she exceptional or
just a little more than "meh"? Things were never clear. "One day, you'll age
out of the Scandinavian hotness," Oliver, one of her mean exes had said.
But that did mean she *was* hot? And yes, the expiration date for women was
so much shorter than for men.

When she was being fitted for her wedding dress at the Bridal
Warehouse, the woman on the pedestal next to her in the group fitting
room was attractive, slim, thirties, maybe even early forties but still young
looking in a dress cascading with tiers of crinoline making her look like a
wedding cake herself. The top was a bejeweled bustier that showed off her
smooth shoulders. They seemed to be having trouble zipping it, however.

"Hon, we're going to have to let it out," the fitter mumbled through
pins in her mouth.

The woman looked like she was going to cry as the fitter declared
in her cigarette-burred voice, "Perimenopause can add an inch to the back
in just a week. I see it all the time. Changes the whole shape."

Melody's mother used to point out, observationally, when moms
on their block, on some single designated day in their life, changed from

women to linebackers. She stopped pointing it out the day the telephone repair guy saw her from the back, luscious Texas cheerleader mane now short from chemo regrowth, and called her "Mister." Older women were a preview, making Melody more and more aware that for each day that passed, her biggest non-renewable natural resource — her blond blue-eyed beauty, her amply busted body — would all, at some point, dry up and crumble like a sponge forgotten under the sink. She needed time. To consider these fleeting, still-young days. She spent them, possibly unwisely, behind a counter in a hotel attached to a mall in a small city that would just be a town if not for the university.

***

At breakfast, while she was wondering if her headache was from blood pooling into the crevices of her brain, Caleb had brought up "starting a family" again. "No pressure," he said, eyeing her birth control pills. In the kitchen he made her a protein smoothie in which he snuck in a tablespoon of ground flax as if she wouldn't notice the sawdust taste. He also reminded her that the high-folic acid prenatal vitamins were prescription only and should he call Dr. Blair for her? Did she know that potatoes had no B vitamins and that's why Ireland had some of the highest rates of neural tube defects in the world? Neural tubes sounded like something Caleb worked on in his lab.

She had noticed recently that Caleb basically made all the decisions — which cable subscription to buy, where to go on vacation. She had veto power. Like the other night in bed he'd put his hands around her neck. She'd been shocked. She'd said no. He'd stopped, but he seemed mad, or disappointed. Maybe she was a little disappointed in herself, too. Didn't she want to lead a wild life? Be sexually free, try it all? Avoid becoming one of those boring marrieds who do it missionary like once a year? The list of things she didn't know how she felt about was growing, not diminishing. Her head hurt.

What she did know was that she didn't want to fall into having kids, the way so many of her friends did, mostly when they worked a little bit and decided they hated their jobs and you couldn't just "stay home" unless you had a baby to stay home with you. The trouble was, you couldn't know if you didn't want to have kids until after you had them — and then it was too late.

Caleb smoothed his shirt, which she had ironed like a good wifey. She had refrained from chatting so he could listen to his podcast. Today's was about how the presidential nominees from both parties ranted daily about "the common man" while secretly owning shell companies bursting with millions, maybe even billions, serial notebook numbers lined up literally next to each other in some closet in the Caribbean.

"Turk and Caicos, I bet," she said, automatically.

"How'd you know?" Caleb said, impressed. She liked impressing him.

"You look nice," she said to Caleb, his Clark Kent glasses and his floppy forelock — adorable. He smiled, slightly, and nodded.

"Glad you don't have to go out of town for this one," she said. "I'd miss you."

He came over to where she was, pushed her against the wall and smashed his tongue in her mouth in a way that said, *we'll have sex on Saturday night.*

Emboldened, she told Caleb about a TikTok she'd just seen: a fiftyish guy had a goal to save a million frequent flier miles for his retirement. He achieved it basically making a mileage run to Mongolia at the very end, but then got cancer and died before he could redeem a single mile. The wife inherited the miles but then *she* immediately got the *same* cancer, and died. She was pleased when Caleb even whistled in appreciation of her story.

"The husband was probably too obsessed with just completing his goal, and the wife manifested her cancer by thinking too much about her husband's cancer," she posited. "Where your mind goes, the energy flows.

Quantum mechanics."

A little of the old spark was reviving, how much she loved to talk to him. They'd met at the college activities fair. He was manning the Cycling Club booth, next to hers at the Future Journalists club, which had been next to the BDSM Club — what a way to start a convo! They'd talked straight for 13 hours (plus, sex!), they loved to recount to others. She remembered thinking, "I'm never going to get sick of this man."

"Ha, that is so *not* how quantum mechanics works."

"Well," she said, stung. "Why don't you tell me how it works, then?"

Caleb didn't answer her. He often didn't these days. Thirty percent of the time, maybe. Even to her own ears, however, her words were excessive. She basically said something, no reply, then answered herself, her voice discordantly tangling and competing with the dudes' on the podcast.

Caleb snapped the laptop shut. She thought it was to listen to her better, but it was to drop it into his briefcase and leave the room.

***

She called an Uber and was actually early, not having to park five blocks away and walk. Paul, today's co-Desk Attendant, huffed up two minutes after SOS — Start of Shift. Paul didn't get fired, probably because he spent his breaks monitoring the security cams. They were manned properly by a security guard after midnight, but during the day they played to an empty room. Management appreciated any "extramural monitoring." Paul's best catch so far had been a Postmates delivery guy peeing in the stairwell. He basically made his creepy Peeping Tom tendencies work for him.

She was settled in, it was showtime. She had two black eyes (coverable with makeup)! Understated shell-shaped earrings, her favorite heels: pumps with tapered coffin-nail heels that looked much higher than they were, a little sexy, even, yet within the corporate-mandated 1.5-2.0-inches. She hoped she looked promotable. Today was a convention booking, so it would be busy. Today:

USA Little Miss Dance, Dance Revolution

Conventions were more than half their bookings, but for them at the desk it was awful. First, they were swarmed all at once, especially if the Westin on the other end of the mall was sold out and they got the overflow. Then there was the internecine competition over who got the better room.

Once, a Black guy complained about his room, so she finessed an upgrade. He reappeared five minutes later, visibly steaming. PREMIUM GROUND FLOOR turned out to be a semi-basement with a single window like a porthole on a ship. She'd never been in that room and indeed, looking at the photos on his phone, it looked like a storage room. But when would *she* ever actually be inside a guest room? The DAs were forbidden to set foot in the *lobby* in uniform after shift. She'd had to grab her Ubers over by the mall.

Of course that guy pulled his Race Card. Jose hurriedly turbo-charged his upgrade to the King suite that cost $800 retail and gave him extra Bonvoy points (as historic as the Arcade looked, it was still owned by Marriott). But Jose's apology on "my staff's behalf" felt unfair. She'd done her job, followed the corporate handbook to a T. If this had happened more recently, she would have become an infamous TikTok villian under the "Karens Gone Wild" genre; at least she could be thankful this had happened before everyone filmed every little interaction. She wasn't racist.

The dance moms demanded early check-in, and either looked hopeless or angry when she told them they were welcome to put their bags in the store-room. When she snuck looks at them, skin already bumpy and leathery, balayage blond streaks to distract from the encroaching gray frizzies, their horny (in a bad way) feet in sandals, she couldn't help thinking, how can a woman *do* that to herself? They look so haggard now, what will they look like when their kids are in college?

Watching the rigamarole of the luggage roundup, the whining, Melody was brought back to how her mom, solo after their dad died when she was twelve, somehow got her and Danny to Disneyland, the Grand Canyon. She was a teacher and so busy all year. Didn't she ever just secretly want to say fuck it and have a nice summer to herself? She signed all their school forms, attended PTAs, then came home and did the dishes, even as they whined for not liking dinner (now she understood why her mom melted down or couldn't get out of bed from time to time).

Melody distinctly remembered being eight, feeling a little off, crawling into her parents' bed. So nice and warm. Then she'd unexpectedly thrown up *and* had diarrhea. Her father had leapt out of the bed and run away.

But her mother had bathed her, washed her hair. Piped Tylenol into her feverish mouth. Thrown the fouled bedding into the machine at two a.m., scrubbed the mattress where the acidic vomit and liquified shit had soaked through while Dad snored on the couch. The whole time no complaint, not even a sigh of exhaustion because her mother never wanted anyone to feel bad. Her mom was great. No doubt. When she died, what would they put on her headstone?

MOM
She was great.

No different than a zillion other moms, unremembered by the rest of the world.

Melody considered this mathematically and concluded she still had time. With egg freezing and stuff, fertility could go on way after forty. Fifty was *twenty* years away. But she wished she could try it on for a day. Being a fifty-year-old mom. Or at least have an older woman answer honestly: were you just toodling along, being young and hot and then did it just creep up on you and catch you unawares like a mountain lion jumping on a jogger? What did you wish *you* had done with those years?

Her nights recently had consisted of watching TikToks or Netflix. She and her married friends from college never talked anymore, especially if they had kids. Scrolling and TV was beginning to feel hollow, so she had lately been going to bed at nine just to make a hopefully more interesting tomorrow get here faster. Would she look back and hit herself realizing she'd *kill* to go back to this very boring day? That at eighty she would be *ecstatic* to do this again for even five minutes, where right now, she couldn't stand printing out yet another bag tag for even five minutes longer?

A few of her friends were divorced already. Almost all of those were from cheating (both sides, but more men than women). In some ways she envied the clarity that would bring. If Caleb ever cheated, she would be so out of there.

The one thing she never had to wonder about, however, was if he was cheating. When he got in his romantic moods, he often said things like, "You're my one and only." She handled the cringe by joking that she couldn't have an affair, either, she was just too lazy, it would take too long to explain herself to someone new. But she could also feel in her bones that Caleb was true, and faithful. He taught "sections," which were like classes that the professor fobbed off on his grad students, and of course he had groupies. Girls who would wear mini skirts and open their legs in class. But she never worried. His phone could ping and light up all day and she never had even the slightest urge to peer over at it. This was, any way you sliced it, a positive. An absence of added stress.

But was that what she had signed up for? Partnering for less stress and not demanding more of life?

Their senior year, they'd both been excited for "real life" to begin. Then, out of the ten PhD programs he'd applied to, Caleb got into only one — the one already at their school, that his prof helped him get into. They went out to dinner to celebrate nonetheless.

Contemplating the dessert cart, she hadn't even noticed that Caleb had gotten on one knee and flipped open a box in which lay a sparkly ring from Zales, in her correct size. She had thought for the first twenty seconds of the proposal, though she would never admit it, he was crouched there to get a better look at the petit-fours. Suddenly, the whole restaurant, packed with Friday night revelers, was invested in them. Dozens of eyeballs on them, the "Say yes! Say yes!" chants. She'd moved as if in a fog. Made emotive noises. She'd said "yes" (to cheers) practically like a safe word just to wipe the eyes off her. Just like how she'd said "I love you," when he'd said it to her the first time, because you couldn't really just reply with silence. You just couldn't.

She honestly hadn't expected to be engaged. She was 22! She had always thought of 28 as the perfect age to get married. How was she going to tell Caleb she'd already paid for ResumeX.com, to "be seen by thousands of companies!!!" and checked off pharma, advertising, retail — almost all of the companies in New York, LA, or Chicago; exactly zero near their dumpy lake-effect college town.

One of the drug companies actually called saying they were impressed with her CV and would she be interested in taking a writing test. They sent her journal articles about an imaginary drug with an equally imaginary name: Billoyornazeb, and she was supposed to write an editorial ("advertorial") whose goal was to help Billoyornazeb become the next blockbuster drug. Challenge accepted!

She used a thesaurus to not repeat common words. She studied the graphs with the number of patients in the study ($n = 183$) while dreaming about licking the frilled icing from a Magnolia cupcake and having a cute apartment. The finished piece praised Billoyornazeb's "outstanding effectiveness on post-exertional malaise, including for COVID-19 and its sequelae" while, as instructed, gently skipping over the few really bad side effects, like thickening of the heart wall.

In the meantime, she equally gently broached the idea of a long engagement, maybe even long distance! She thought Caleb would want to sit down and discuss it like rational people with healthy communication did; instead, he stormed out of the room and went to stay with friends. The silent treatment went on for a week. She was relieved when he finally texted her. *U up?*

After they had sex, good sex, she decided now was the time to push. "Honestly, what's the hurry?" Lying on her back, looking at the ceiling, she'd been twisting the diamond ring on her finger, thinking she'd return it to him, depending on his answer.

"I didn't think you were *that* kind of person," he'd said, slowly, into the dark.

"What kind of person?" Caleb's dad was a professor. His whole family always seemed like they knew what they were doing, how to *be*, and undoubtedly this was a knowledge Caleb had. She wanted some of that.

"Flighty. Problems with commitments. I want this to work. I'm not so sure you do, though."

"No, no," she protested. But the "no" really was more a reflex — she needed to bring the mood up. Men brooded. Women cheered them up. "It's not that."

"Then what is it?"

She tried to stammer out how it would be *good* for the relationship. It would make them both surer. *If you love something, let it go* — that poster her mom had. *If it comes back to you, it's yours. If it doesn't, it never was yours to begin with.*

He shook his head. "You understand I'm making big life plans. Not just for me, for *us*. I really want this to work."

"I do, too," she insisted but without knowing what "to work" would look like.

"I don't think you do. I don't think you understand about investing in relationships."

"I do," she said. And to prove it, she removed herself from all her ResumeX interviews, including the one at the drug company in New York, the writing job.

Then her mother got COVID. She got better thanks to some new drug — whose name Melody recognized because it sounded like Beelzebub: Billoyornazeb. *Billoyornazeb!* "The drug with outstanding effectiveness for post-exertional malaise." Those were *her* words. Why was she not in New York City, writing these all day and rewarding herself with Magnolia cupcakes per thousand words?

Moving to this new city for his post-doc at least gave her a larger field.

She even joined a few meetups in her town with the double duty of maybe making some female friends. Pottery. Birdwatching. Stargazing at the Pozzi Observatory at the university! All tepidly fun. Forget men, when she saw a woman she thought was cool and said, "We should hang out sometime," she'd get a panicked look like she was a Mormon trying to convert them. The stargazing night had been heartbreakingly clean and pure and it had smelled nice outside. But everyone there was either an old person with their comfy friends or a couple on date night. She thought the single, gay guy would be a sure thing, but he scuttled away when she'd asked him if he'd figured out which planet was Jupiter. She even invited Caleb to these outings and had to admit, it was more relaxing to have someone "there" for you. On TikTok, it seemed so many women pined for a guy just to pay *some* attention to her. And here she had Caleb, who would never cheat. Would she later think she was delulu, having all that, and then just throwing it away to be alone...and unhappy again?

She signed up for a writer's workshop at the library. She'd had secret dreams of becoming a journalist, but that had seemed so far-fetched she'd never told anyone. Her one application to journalism school, at Columbia in New York (New York!) was rejected, and it had been impossible to tell if she'd just missed it or if they'd been laughing at her application. She had been president of the journalism club, but didn't have any writing to share as a sample. Truth be told, she hated "cold" interviewing people, but felt like once she was established, she could just force herself to do it. Now, she been doing a little writing on her own. She even wrote a Letter to the Editor, in which she used facts and statistics like she had for the Billoyornazeb advertorial. They never got back to her. Which she took as confirmation from the universe. Writing/journalism was not for her. She needed to find a gig, a job, it didn't have to be a passion product. What's an attractive woman to do? Guest Associate was something she basically fell into.

***

Paul was almost always on the day shift with her, but today it was Tricia. Tricia was somehow attending law school while working here full time. As usual, hair was immaculate in a sleek ballerina bun. When she reported for duty, she was *on*, like those actors who never break out of character even at lunch. Melody could envision her moving easily from here to court with her no nonsense, slightly terrifying mien. Her skin was beautiful and smooth but she seemed much older than her. She never wore any signifying jewelry on her hands.

ROOFING AND VENTURE CAPITAL EXPO was today's convention.

She and Tricia looked at the sign. "Is that two conventions or one?" she wondered. Roofing suggested older dudes, like forties, bad ties, the alkali smell of sweat, middle-aged paunches, they were generally not too much trouble. But venture cap. That meant young cocky dudes. Probably mad that their convention was being held in such an uninteresting, middling city. The King suite *and* the penthouse were indeed sold out.

"Are you a model?" said the next customer.

She kept her eyes demurely averted. She had trained herself not to make a cringe face. She glanced at his driver's license. Young guy, about her age. Brad Chesebrough.

During their DA orientation, the first powerpoint slide

**BETWEEN THE TIMES OF CHECK IN AND CHECK OUT
THE GUEST IS KING**

As manager, Jose was the only one allowed to yell at people or kick them out.

"*Are* you a model?"

Why, she wondered, should she have to endure mid-level flirtation if she wasn't paid for it? At least the baristas or whatever got to have a tip jar. She certainly deserved compensation for suffering under the "male gaze" (a term she had picked up at one of Caleb's grad school parties).

"I'm sure with a face like that you'll make it big soon."

"The wi-fi is free, the password is in the folder. If you want 5-G it's an extra $15 per day, Mr. Chesebrough." She did not smile. "Frigid bitch," he muttered under his breath as he left.

She was regretting letting him check in early, though it was more for her convenience than his. She did some silent deep breathing to temper her annoyance, reminding herself that she was the fixed person in what was a transitory space for everyone else. That people had their best and worst behaviors while traveling. (Hm: "fixed person in what was a transitory space for others"—that was pretty good! She wrote that down). She had indeed gotten good at leaving a professionally neutral look on her face while letting her conscious self fly up into the ceiling and look down with amusement and snide commentary. A great skill especially for when people started to bluster about her not being able to find their reservation… because they hadn't made one at all and were just trying to bluff their way into a last-minute room.

Four o'clock, official check in time, a forty-something guy cold shouldered Tricia (because she was Black?) and strode right to her. Unlike the dance moms, he had aged nicely like wine, his tan gilded by shining hairs as he popped his cuff to write something down. Cordial, not smarmy, strong square jaw. He had the kind of unrecognizable watch that she suspected cost more than the houses she and Caleb were looking at on Zillow lately. The guy with him — sharing the King Suite — had expensively manipulated five o'clock shadow. They were joined by a bald guy who had vroomed up in a fancy car with two exhaust pipes, coal-rolling the valets.

"Eyyyyy you got the rumpus room!" Baldy said. It was cringe when older people acted young, the contrast between his sk8trboi hoodie and sneakers with this bald and eyebrowless head didn't help. He immediately slunk off and lit a cigar behind a fern in the lobby and laughed when he tripped the smoke alarm. He shook security off to walk outside with his stogie. When asked to write down the license plate of his car he wrote CRYPTO and she didn't know if it was a joke. She had to admit, there was something attractive about that kind of confidence, especially from someone who looked like *that*. She wondered what he'd look like in a serious power suit (haha while men undressed women in their minds, women secretly *dressed* men).

What would it be like if he were her husband, not Caleb?

She should stop that. Thinking about running away with each guy she met.

But how would she know if she deserved better, without comparison, better/worse?

Or, was she just stirring up useless chaos. After their fights Caleb would look at her with something like pity and declare "you just seem sad for some unknowable reason."

***

The King Suites bros returned to the lobby and sat in the plush chairs, waiting. They were joined by the "are you a model?" guy. Cheese-bro.

Feeling she could use a little bit of a pick-me-up, she had smiled directly and brightly at him when he re-entered the lobby, but he had walked right by her. A flame shot up from her liver. She knew it was dumb, but she was insulted.

A bevy of tall, gorgeous women in up-dos walked in the door. They did not stop at the desk but just linked up with the dudes, one for each. There was something funny going on. Was it misogynist of her to think they might be prostitutes? Especially because, Tricia told her, the men had also rented out one of the smaller conference rooms "The Sunset Room," for some mysterious conference business. Cheese-bro was looking at his date like he was hungry and she was a piping hot hamburger.

"They asked if the doors locked," Tricia said, allowing herself a rare eyeroll. "Saying they were discussing top secret business stuff."

Many things went on in these rooms. They had doors that locked, no windows, but hello it was still "public" hotel space for which they were allowed to have surveillance. During a plastic surgery conference, she and Paul and even Jose had all squeezed into the surveillance room to watch a woman lying on a banquet table in the Travis Mills Ballroom; a doctor in a bad suit injected her face with something then pierced the skin of her cheek with a huge needle and ran a thread or a wire under her face skin and pulled it tight like a marionette. The other doctors all took notes.

One more break before it was time to go home. She slipped into the surveillance room for one last peek at the Sunset Room. Lights dimmed, dudes in the corners, run of the mill hand and BJs. She never saw money changing hands because if she did that would be an excuse to tell Jose. Maybe cement her Assistant General Manager promotion, that is, if she wanted it.

She reviewed the cams: elevator, hall, lobby. Wait, what was this? Cheese-bro was literally cornering one of the young maids in an empty hall. He wasn't touching her, but from her terrified face, he was saying disgusting things to her.

The guest is king. What a load of crap. Calling them guests was a load of crap. Guests are considerate in your house. They don't demand you pay attention to them and then also ignore you. She pulled up Facebook on her phone. Cheese-bro was not a common name.

PROUD Christian
Husband
Shannon is the love of my life. She is my life's greatest blessing, as are our

Cheese-bro had, earlier, used the hotel messaging system to text the front desk to complain about a spider in his room. She wrote down the cell number, which was the same one on Facebook — set to public. It was simple to find the other three dude-bros: all proudly listed ROOFING AND VENTURE CAPITAL in their bios. Baldy's profile picture was of him with his car, showing its plate, indeed CRYPTO. They all of course had gorgeous wives and girlfriends. What, did dude-bros believe they were so on top of the world they could never get caught either by their wives or the SEC? When she googled them, it turned out each one of them, including Nice Watch, had rich parents. They were "venture capitalists," which basically meant they got to play with dad's money.

She barely saved her wages especially after dry cleaning her uniforms, her expensive shoes, now her money pit of a car. She was always trying to get Caleb to consider how were they were going to afford a house *and* a baby? Caleb acted like she didn't know how to do math. She knew too well that the odds of having a happy, unstressed, enjoyable life were stacked against them.

About the only way to monetize if you didn't have daddy money was to access a special skill or product. She wished she knew how to create an app or monetize her looks on the internet. How did that young woman *in Korea* become a zillionaire just by posting videos of herself eating ginormous amounts of food (and not even being particularly attractive) but having a kind of porny, deep-throated way of eating? She hadn't even considered something like influencing or Youtube because the old people in their "career" office could barely use "the internets" and scared her about having a gap in her resume, "No one will hire you!" That's why she felt like she *had* to take the hotel job when it was offered. Like, what did Seth Dimas do in that time when he was noodling around for years and developing SKOOTr? Clearly not worrying about gaps in his resume!

***

It was raining. Mindful of her shoes, instead of calling the Uber right away, she took the skyway to the mall Rite-Aid. She loved mall drug stores because since they didn't have an actual pharmacy, they made up for it by selling odd and wondrous junk: souvenirs of their mid-list town (the Travis Mills snow-globe), pumpkin spice Tic Tacs, adorably teeny-tiny tubs of Vaseline. A whole glassed-in display of "disposable" phones. Phones were disposable now! This one even had a camera--and a voice activated assistant named Jenna!

She bought the Tic Tacs, and a phone plus a $50 plan that came as a card that you scratched off the foil like for the lottery. This is what women needed burner phones for. Not for affairs, but to yank their lives back before it's too late. To document control group Melody. The one who never said "yes" to Caleb that night in the Wagon Wheel. Maybe she'd start a burner Insta account to see what this other life looked like, and maybe it would help her gather the courage to go after it. She also bought a miniature tub of Vaseline because she liked it. She might have liked something for her headache, but that Costco bottle of ibuprofen waited at home. She also realized she hadn't eaten her lunch, which was still in the employee fridge, in its ugly bag.

She encountered no one when looping back through the employee entrance. The surveillance room was deserted, so she went into it to check on what was the action in the Sunset Room. Dark. They must have gone out. She rewound the latest footage. Cheese-bro of course was the most enthusiastic of the bros. However, Handsome Nice Watch guy was, to her disappointment, a volunteer firefighter, married *and* a BJ enthusiast. She paused it at Cheese-bro's face clenched mid-orgasm.

All the dudes' women just seemed like nice women. Stubble's wife was a SAHM. Baldy's wife was some kind of beauty entrepreneur. Shannon was, get this - a divorce lawyer.

On a whim, she took a picture of the screen. She felt strangely powerful. She had something on these dudes. Evidence was money in the bank. But more than money, she wanted to help people. If she were Shannon, wouldn't she want some front desk clerk to anonymously tip her off?

When Facebook was new, Melody accidentally created two accounts, but now she used the dormant one, which was just titled Melodeeeeee, to DM the beautiful Shannon: *do you think knowledge is power?*

She was thinking of adding, *NOT a Nigerian scam!* But that would actually make it seem like a scam for sure.

I sure do! Shannon messaged back with surprising openness.

Viewing her Facebook, Melody discerned that unless Shannon was hiding some kind of double life, all she ever did was work, shepherd the daughters to their ballet lessons (unlike the Cheese, sloppy with his private data, she meticulously covered the faces of her daughters with rainbow unicorn emoji stickers), planned a huge 40th birthday party in Bali for him. Shannon must be blinded by love. She must see cheaters all day long at her law practice. She just trusted Cheese-bro! When she shouldn't! Melody sent Shannon the orgasm picture, nothing X-rated—it could just be him sneezing or having a seizure in another context. And felt virtuous. Like a kind of Mother Theresa.

Where's Shannon? she DMed the Cheese impulsively.

WHO IS THIS appeared immediately—even faster than Shannon's reply. *Do u have more?*

Guilty! Her fiendish fingers had a mind of their own.

I have pictures !!! !!!!!

She said in her DM first to wife, then husband.

…

WHAT DO YOU WANT?!?!?! (Him)

I don't need anything more (Her)

Melody's bag felt heavy with secrets as she went back through the skyway to the mall's second floor from whose one-way glass she had a clear view to the hotel's front door. She had a long coat on, so only her coffin-nailed shows were visible, and she took a moment to appreciate how chic they looked, her slim ankles, no sign of cankles yet. Under her toe: a dime.

Her burner phone lit up. Each were sent instructions to withdraw $500 cash each and meet in front of the hotel. It was fun to see them run out, shielding their eyes against the rain, looking for whomever. Looking for her. They deserved at least a little stress in their lives. *Cash, or the pictures go straight to the wifey.*

She hadn't 100% thought this through, of course. Jump scare was worth something, but she probably could never get the cash. She wished she knew how that crypto stuff worked. Caleb was always acting like that was something women were too dumb to understand. She wasn't *that* dumb. She just wasn't interested. A little googling on her phone. It seemed too ridiculous to deal with the 32-digit strings of numbers ("the blockchain"). But then she found not one but several apps that — ha! — let you make accounts without ID. She made a bunch of accounts to make up for the fact the amount of cash she could receive per transaction was small. While she was at it, she also requested cash from Shannon. Only as a "tip" and "karma." Shannon tipped generously and immediately, which made Melody ask for that same amount from the bros: *in addition.*

Cheese-bro was gesticulating to Baldy, Baldy was grabbing Stubble by the lapels. She sent a text reminding them of the deadline, five minutes. Nice Watch (a.k.a. Handsome Volunteer Firefighter and BJ Enthusiast) wasn't there. Maybe he was pawning his watch at the pawn shop behind the mall.

Ding! Came one.

Ding!

Another.

Ding! Ding!

These guys got to party and cheat on their company's dime. They weren't even going to miss this money. She felt like that guy on the show, the one who made a vigorous, Robin Hood-ish living stealing from drug dealers. He was also Buddhist and said he never took any excess, just what he needed to live. What a great plan — what were they going to do, go to the police?

The cherry on top, she sent the pictures to Shannon. She made sure to get a little bit of the maid footage in there as well. This woman had daughters. Maybe the others did, too. She predicted Cheese-bro would get a call within thirty seconds. Indeed, he took the call, clutched his head, started running in place, all the excess adrenaline. Her work here was done.

She made sure to exit via the far corner of the mall, her cloche hat obscuring her face. The rain was sluicing off the roof, swirling in whirlpools around the drain. She had no umbrella because she was Ubering. Her shoes felt soggy and cold and started to fill with rain. With the wind spitting rain in her face, she could barely see, and those damn kitten heels made her wobble. She ducked into the partial relief of a bus shelter. Her loosely belted trench did nothing against the sharp drop in temperature.

From the far end of the shelter, she heard a snuffling sound and thought it must be a raccoon but no, a disheveled man was balanced on the end of the bench, dreaming. It must have been a good dream, he was smiling, his hands vigorously moving in his pants. His shoes, incongruously, looked expensive, and were placed neatly and precisely next to his prone body.

AIRPORT said the bus pulling up. She reached out her arm, waved.

She boarded. The rain, now mixed with ice, tinkled on the windows. The bus plowed through the rising water, a comforting shushing sound beneath the wheels.

She and Caleb kept a joint account for house expenses. Caleb still owed her from when, years ago, the grad students went on strike, failed, and he didn't get his stipend. Every six months she'd reminded him, and each time he'd get mad over her being "trivial." She flipped open her wallet to make sure the ATM card was in it.

She was realizing her temples no longer throbbed just as they passed by Madwell's Ave, the area upwind of the mall where the naughty businesses were. Zazu's Porn Superstores! Lady Godiva. Buns and Roses - unlimited buffet!

Then they continued to Reservoir Hill with all the fancy restaurants. The hill transitioned into a neighborhood where, unlike the stately Tudor houses near campus, the houses were vinyl-sided and quirky, a number of them flew giant, soggy political flags. The insides of the houses looked warm and yellow like lit jack o'lanterns.

In all of these places, she thought. Women were working. While their kids were growing up with devices stuck in their hands, bossing around Siri or Jenna or whatever, being trained from birth to view women as secretaries, maids, assistants.

She slipped her regular phone into the dirty looking slot between the seat and the window. It fell several feet with a reassuring thunk.

Would Caleb see "her" navigating the city, going in slow circles to nowhere, thinking what's my crazy chaos wife up to now? At the airport, after googling, *Can you buy a plane ticket with cash? What airlines go to Turks & Caicos?* she'd smear the Tracphone's buttons with Vaseline to hide fingerprints and toss it somewhere.

The rain tap-tap-tapped like a baby's fingernails on the plexiglass. The drops juddered and split, forming Ys on the way down that reconstituted to Xs then back to Ys. Catching the outside lights, the pattern on the window looked unreal and alien in its reds and oranges and greens. Mesmerized, she wondered how she had missed this beauty, missed herself, all this time.

Signs

by Joshua Shapiro

It is her favorite part of the day, except for the pain. The bed is high and getting into it is hard on her knees. Tonight her son stays with her. He stays too long.

"Are you comfortable?" he says.

"Very comfortable, thank you."

"We had a good day."

"It was a lovely day."

"I think we all enjoyed the movie. Kirsten laughed all the way through it."

"Was it a funny movie?" she says, and knows she has made a mistake.

"You laughed too, Ma."

She doesn't remember. She has something like a memory of the three of them in the warm room with the fireplace and the enormous television. Was she laughing? All she can bring to mind is the news, nothing to laugh at there, just angry people. People waving signs, people shouting from the windows of cars, people who paint messages on sheets they hang from buildings. Perfectly good linen ruined. What she does remember is the television set in her parlor, her mother's parlor, a much smaller set of course but there was always something worth a laugh. That Danny Thomas.

"Tomorrow you have an appointment with Doctor Giles," he says.

"Another appointment?" she says, glad he dropped the other embarrassing business.

"You haven't had your feet looked at in a couple of months."

"I thought —"

She thought the one called Giles was an eye doctor. Someone is.

She sees doctors for her bladder, knees, heart, eyes, and of course the other condition. A mental condition. They have a name for it that she can't recall. No matter. In her day people didn't talk about such things.

Her son is on the bed now, sitting on the edge the way her mother used to before tucking her in and turning out the light. As she herself did for her son when he was a small boy. She is not nostalgic, and has no wish to be treated like a child. If he would just leave she could enjoy this, the best part of the day. She could stop working so hard. It is hard work pretending to understand what everyone is constantly saying to her. Mostly it is the wife. She is nice enough but can't seem to let a grown woman live her own life.

Finally he bends to kiss her cheek. The door is closed, the room is dark. Her knees no longer hurt. She usually suffers from several lesser pains and at the moment can find none of them. It feels as if she has just put down a heavy shopping bag she's been carrying around all day. The bed is soft and fragrant, and in it the present slips away. Good riddance. She can live again. She can be the office manager in Mr. Falcone's drapery firm. She can be a wife making the avocado and cheese dip, always a success. She can be a young mother, dress for the PTA, drive her boy to baseball practice. She can be the schoolgirl and put on the plaid skirt and walk the five blocks to Blessed Sacrament Academy. She can —

Some time passes. The house is very quiet. She does not have to use the toilet but she will, just in case. Another accident would be humiliating. When she opens the door to the bathroom and turns on the light, she is surprised to see it full of clothing. It is her clothing and she wonders who put it in the bathroom, arranged so neatly on hangers and shelves. And here is her favorite robe! She slips it on over her pajamas. She knots the belt and steps into the slippers with the soft fleece. She feels ready to take on the world, as she used to. The world is not in here, so she opens first the bedroom door and then the front door. It is good that she sleeps on the first floor. She won't disturb anyone.

They live at the corner of Jackson and Myrtle. This information is on the lamppost and she tries to memorize it. By the time she reaches the corner of Jackson and Elm she has forgotten. No matter. She is warm enough in her robe. Her knees are hurting but not too much, and she isn't worried about a fall. Between the moon and the streetlights she can see every crack and bump. She can see the houses, not quite as handsome on this block although the flower beds all have the same sign. It is a blue sign on a stick in the dirt. *Tolerance,* it says.

From an open window comes music, or whatever they call music these days. It is one of those singers who doesn't actually sing, just recites fast rhymes. The singer is one of them. She is not prejudiced, she never has been. They had that President and he seemed like a nice man. His picture is also in front of some of the houses. She thinks her son may have this sign or the other sign or both. She has always been tolerant. She used to put Nat King Cole on the phonograph, they had a Silvertone with the radio built in, she watched her father fix it once with a hot iron and solder. Such a clever man. Suddenly songs were pouring out of the cabinet again but nothing like this new music. The words that she can make out through the window are shameful, and she walks past as quickly as she can.

She nearly walks into a man. A large dark man, not young, standing in the middle of the sidewalk.

"You okay, lady?" he says.

"I am out for a walk, sir, and you are in my path."

"I ain't in nobody's path."

"Are you planning to hurt me?"

"Now why would you be asking me that? Oh yeah, I know why. But just for the record, I don't hurt nobody. I'm just tryin' to be polite to somebody who looks like she might be lost."

"I am *not* lost."

"It's one o'clock in the morning and you're out walkin' around in a bathrobe and slippers. I got an old mama who goes wanderin' off."

"It is not your business, sir, what I choose to wear or where I choose to walk."

She feels clearer than she has in months. A walk is just the thing. So is a little assertiveness. She used to be a force to be reckoned with, back in Mr. Falcone's office. But there is a time and a place, and she has been too hard on this man. He has been kind, and she is not prejudiced. She stands straighter, despite the worsening pain. She draws the sash of her robe tighter, a little embarrassed she did not have the time to dress properly for an outing. She makes sure to speak with the formal precision of her class.

"I am grateful for your concern, sir, but my health requires that I walk a certain amount every day. Day or night. Night or day. In my time I was something of an athlete. I had an opportunity to go to Bryn Mawr. My son is an accountant. I am telling you this because I myself planned to study accounting —"

One part of her hears herself rambling as the other part rambles. The first part wants to stop the second part, but it cannot. To avoid further embarrassment she walks on. The man does not prevent her. She hears him call after her.

"You be careful, now, lady. I hope you're not plannin' to go the other side. They be trouble on the other side."

She pays no attention. Or she does but cannot understand his meaning, and she's lived in this city all her life. Unless he means the highway, that ugly thing on rusting trestles. When she was in high school she watched the highway being built. There were shops in the way that they knocked down. At least the school is still there. Here it is beside her, wide steps and columns and Latin words above the entrance. It must be for younger children now, the windows are decorated with glitter. Each window contains a huge silver letter that together spell out the single word *Tolerance.*

With difficulty she walks along the quiet main street. She is hungry and Bachmann's Deli always has the best pastrami. And here it is, right where it's supposed to be, she could find any of these places blindfolded, nothing wrong with her sense of direction. Except it isn't a deli, it's a yoga studio. Next to it is the shop where her parents bought the Silvertone. The first time she ever saw a television it was right here, behind this window. The small flickering picture made her late for supper on more than one occasion. The window is still here but the display contains a machine that looks like a big copper drum. The contraption gleams. Beside it are a few open burlap sacks full of coffee beans. In a dimly lit case in back are pastries that make her mouth water. Paper signs are tacked to a cork board in the entrance alcove. *Mindful Meditation,* says one. *Stop Killing the Planet,* says another. There is an invitation to become a member of the Gay/Lesbian/ Trans Alliance. Precisely what this is she cannot say, but she knows enough. She wasn't born yesterday.

The highway is as busy at this late hour as at any hour. Beneath the overpass a man with filthy gray hair and beard is asleep sitting up with a liquor bottle in his hand. Her father drank in the evenings. By the time she went to college, not Bryn Mawr but the Mildred Webb Secretarial School, he drank also in the mornings. They had a television set themselves by then. It had broken and stayed broken in the corner of their living room. This was in the house on Muncie Street. She is sure it is somewhere near here, on this side. When they built the highway they split the town in two. Over here there is a different sound and a different smell. Neither is pleasant.

The shops too are different. Iron mesh has been rolled down over the doors of the closed establishments. Through the caged fronts she sees a store that sells parts for cars, a liquor store, a locksmith, a gun shop. In every window is a sign. It says *Freedom.* A brick wall is painted to show men with helmets and rifles in camouflage uniforms. The picture's caption, in huge red, white, and blue letters, is also this one word, *Freedom.* And hovering above the soldiers is the face of the other man who was President, the one with orange hair. The picture frightens her. It's as if the entire building is angry, the way the television in her son's house is always angry. The television in her girlhood home had never been angry, when it worked. Ozzie and Harriet were more than enough for people. There was no noisy highway dividing the town, no violent pictures on buildings, no strange Alliances.

She walks away from the brick mural the way she walked away from the drunk beneath the trestles, quickly and painfully. She is trying to decide which is worse, the pain, the fear, or the hunger. She can not decide because all of a sudden, from out of nowhere, a young man is running at her. He wears camouflage like the men in the wall painting. He is hardly more than a boy. He has no gun but he has a stubby black club. She sees the stitching on it as the boy runs past. She is recovering from the shock when another boy, this one wearing dungarees and a leather jacket, appears from the same hidden place. It is an alley behind the painted wall.

This boy stops when he sees her. He stands at a respectful distance and looks her up and down in a puzzled way. Then he looks over his shoulder, at the alley.

"It isn't safe out here, Ma'am."

"I have no intention of remaining out here."

"I can walk you home if you want."

"That will not be necessary," she says. Old pride makes her say it. Again she has the feeling of two parts of herself refusing to cooperate.

"You live on this side?" he asks.

"I live…I live…not far." She strains to recall a street name. A tree of some kind, or a President. But what comes to mind is a place, and she says, "I live on Muncie Avenue."

"That's just a couple of blocks. Let me walk with you. There's Reds everywhere tonight."

She allows him to take her arm. He is tall and strong, and still breathing hard from running. And he is very young, younger than she thought. A good boy. When she stumbles on the crumbling concrete he supports her, as a gentleman would.

"When I was a girl this was a nice, family neighborhood," she says.

"Like, no Reds at all?"

"Are you referring, young man, to communists?"

"I wouldn't know. I mean people like them."

Speaking softly, he points to a cottage beside them, with unfinished timbers holding up the roof and cinder blocks for steps. It is dark and silent.

"I see no people," she says.

"You can always tell from the signs," says the boy.

In the flower bed by the cinder blocks, where no flowers grow, or plants of any kind for that matter, is indeed a sign. It sits crookedly on a stick, the same size and in the same spot as the signs on the other side of the highway. Except this one says *Freedom.*

"You know," he says, "the Reds and the Blues. I'm a Blue. We protest and we argue, and sometimes we fight. Tonight one of them biffed me. That's why I was chasing him. Why I got this."

He takes from his pocket a gun.

"Someone your age has no business with one of these things," she says.

"Everyone my age has one, just about. Younger kids, even. It's totally legal now. Hey, where are you going, Muncie is this way."

But it is this way, she is certain of it, and with her remaining strength she leads him. They are soon walking towards a block of houses slightly larger and slightly better kept.

"So you're not on Muncie?" he says.

"I certainly am," she says. "Number forty-four Muncie Avenue. My father is the building inspector. I have a brother in the service. He is in the Pacific. He sent a letter with the hair from a Japanese soldier. I have been making cookies, ginger bread. Also mincemeat pies. I sell them at the school bazaar. When my brother gets back —"

She has stopped before a house, bigger than a cottage and with brick steps. The clear part of her manages this time to stop the rambling.

"This is Cincinnati Street, not Muncie Avenue," the boy says. "But if this is your house, I'll help you up the stairs. Then I better get going."

"Yeah, you better get going," says a different male voice. It comes from the darkness behind the screen door.

She sees the boy tense, his hand slip into his pocket.

"How about you step away from her," says the voice from the interior.

The boy does not move. He says, very quietly, "Bastard Blue"

The screen door opens and a young man comes out. He is in pajamas. His features are pleasant, almost as pleasant as her son's. Or they would be if they weren't so menacing. She can tell faces. He is a stranger to her, but beneath the glowering there is something comforting about him. He is walking slowly down the few steps. Next to the steps is the *Freedom* sign.

The boy beside her pulls his hand quickly from his pocket. She does not remember many things but she remembers there is a gun in there. The boy draws out only his empty hand and makes a fist. He shakes the fist and runs off, back the way they came.

She is alone with the young man. For some reason she is not afraid.

"You better come in," he says.

She lets him lead her up the steps and into the house.

"Honey, come down!" he calls.

"I'm down already," says a woman's voice.

The woman appears. She has black hair that falls around the neck of her nightgown. Gently she takes the visitor's hand and leads her into the small front room. She seats her in an armchair. It is an embroidered chair. Her mother had a chair like this, and as a child she used to study the pattern on the arms.

"You must be exhausted," the black-haired woman — the wife — says.

"I am very thirsty," the visitor says. She is too polite to say she is hungry.

"I'll get something for you."

The wife goes into the back of the house. Sounds from the kitchen come through the archway. The young man is looking closely at her. He shakes his head sadly. The wife comes back with a glass of juice on a tray.

Also on the tray are several crackers. The visitor was hoping for just such hospitality, and she eats delicately. She sips the juice. This is obviously a home of some refinement.

"I suppose I should call him," the young man says. "I don't want to, but under the circumstances I have to."

"You don't have to because I already did," says the wife.

"What did he say?"

"What do you think he said? That he'll be right over, and that this is the first time she — she went off by herself."

They sit in silence for a time, like a family. There is even, balanced on a table, a television. It is large and flat, so different from the tiny round screen she used to watch through the shop window, or the screen they had at home. She liked to watch from a chair very much like this one. The silence in the room is uncomfortable and she wishes they would turn the television on. Then she thinks better of it.

"Can I get you anything else?" the wife asks her.

"Some aspirin, if it's no trouble."

"We don't have any aspirin but we have something. What hurts?"

"Everything," she says, and laughs.

The wife laughs with her. Then she goes again into the back of the house. The young man does not laugh. He looks very sad. Through the screen door she hears a car pull up. The door of the car opens and closes but the motor is still running. The young man rises but does not otherwise move. The wife has returned with two pink pills and a glass of water, and gives them to her. She is accustomed to taking pills, many pills, without question. She takes these. The young woman puts a hand on her husband's shoulder, by way of encouragement, and he goes to the door. Then she does the same thing for her guest, helping her up and across the room. They stand together on the porch, but not for long. The wife helps her down the steps. Beside the waiting car stands her son.

The older man speaks to the younger man across the distance of the lawn.

"It's been a while," the young man says.

"Too long," says her son.

"She's gotten a lot worse."

"Worse than we realized. We'll have to do something. This won't happen again, I promise."

"Don't worry about it. But how did she find the place?"

"Your guess is as good as mine. Instinct, maybe. Or accident. She grew up not far from here. As you know," her son says.

She knows they are talking about someone, someone they both know and care about. But she doesn't know who. No matter. Her exhaustion is confusing but also freeing. She doesn't want to know. In the moonlight the neighborhood looks peaceful. There are flowers growing in the garden beds in front of every house.

"You used to come here together," says the young man. "All of you."

"We did."

She sees now the resemblance between the men. It gives her a nice feeling.

"That was what?" the young man says. "Seven, eight years ago?"

"At least."

"Well, goodnight, Dad."

"Goodnight."

"Say hi to Mom."

"I will, son."

As they drive off she has never felt so tired. They pass through streets that aren't very nice and then the street with the shops. She sees ghostly figures appear and chase each other around corners and into alleys. Far off is a popping sound, like balloons. They pass beneath an overpass where a disheveled man lies crumpled on the ground, a bottle in his hand. She sees the houses getting more stately. In every garden there is a *Tolerance* sign. It is good to be tolerant. Soon she will be in the soft bed, and she will be free. It is good also to be free. Free to think, free to remember. She will begin by remembering the embroidered chair, the one in the parlor of that nice young man and his wife. It really was just like the chair she used to sit in doing her homework, the Lone Ranger and Lucy, her mother's cookies and her father with his newspaper. That was before the television broke down for good and her brother failed to come home from the Pacific and her father started drinking all the time. The stitching on the arms was exactly the same.

Unaccompanied Minors

by Susan Buttenwieser

It's Sunday night and you are watching television with your brothers and your grandfather is dozing in his brown plaid easy chair when a stranger appears in the living room. Instead of knocking or ringing the bell, the man has let himself in through the door on the side of your grandfather's cottage. You never heard him walking on the gravel road outside, the groan of the rusty hinges when he opened the screen door, or it slapping shut behind him. As if he put some effort into getting inside the cottage without making any noise at all. One minute, it's just the four of you in the living room and then the next, there is also this man.

"Who are *you?*" your little brother, Bear, asks. He lies on top of his green sleeping bag, which is spread out on the floor, wearing only pajama shorts. Although the ceiling fan is turned up high, and there's another one by your grandfather, the living room is thick with July heat-wave heat. Nighttime temperatures have not gone below eighty degrees for days now.

The man doesn't answer Bear's question and towers over your sleeping grandfather. He's turned away so you can't see his face. His thick arms are covered in tattoos and there are more crawling up the back of his neck and onto the base of his bald head. He ignores you and your brothers and, after a long minute of watching your grandfather snoring, flicks him hard on the forehead.

Your grandfather, who you all call Big Daddy, sits upright, rubs his face and opens his eyes, startling when he sees the man. Although he doesn't say hello or introduce the man to you, it's clear he knows him.

"I gotta go to the can, first," Big Daddy says to the tattooed man. He looks scared as he rouses himself out of his chair.

The man continues to act as if you and your brothers aren't there before heading into the kitchen. You hear him open a cupboard and turn on the faucet in the sink as your grandfather flushes the toilet. Big Daddy passes quickly through the living room without looking at you or your brothers. He's got on his baseball cap with a faded B on the front, which he only wears when he's going out somewhere. "Don't wait up for me, I'm gonna be late," he calls to you from the kitchen.

Outside, their footsteps crunch along the road, getting fainter and fainter until they disappear altogether. Then the only sounds are the grasshoppers and crickets and the low din of conversation from the next-door neighbors who are no longer speaking to Big Daddy.

"Where are they going?" Bear asks.

"The IGA," Desmond, your older brother, says with as much certainty as if Big Daddy said so himself. He's sprawled out next to you on the couch and his gaze never leaves the television, yet another old episode of *The Simpsons.*

You don't want to worry Bear, who upsets easily, so you don't say anything. Besides, it seems vaguely possible that Big Daddy is going grocery shopping at nine o'clock at night because there's barely any food in the refrigerator or the cupboards. Even the last of the milk ran out so you have been using a box of long-life for your cereal at breakfast.

Your mother gave Big Daddy an envelope filled with cash when she brought you and your brothers out here to spend all of July at his cottage near Highland Lake. She told him that it was enough to cover the food expenses for the whole time that he's looking after you. After she left, Big Daddy took you to the IGA so you and your brothers could show him what you like to eat. You took the opportunity to select groceries that your mother never allows: Coco Pops, Lucky Charms, Frosted Flakes, Apple Jacks with marshmallows, variety packs of Lay's potato chips, Ruffles, Pringles, Doritos, Cheese Whiz, salami, Marshmallow Fluff, Root Beer, Cherry Coke, Sprite, Super Sweet Iced Tea, Hostess cupcakes, chocolate pudding, Cool Whip, Sara Lee cakes, Double Stuff Oreos, frozen White Castle burgers, frozen waffles, Ben and Jerry's ice cream, an ice cream cake, ice cream sandwiches. And hot dogs, which used to be considered a special treat dinner, something your mother only allowed on weekends or vacation. But you finished off all the other things for dinner after the first week or so, and the hot dogs became the only option. The buns eventually got moldy and had to be thrown out and you used up all the ketchup. So now it's just boiled pink meat night after night, which is close to impossible to chew and swallow all on its own.

You might never be able to eat another hot dog again in your entire life.

You only went grocery shopping with your grandfather that one time, and although he has picked up a few things here and there, occasional gallons of milk, bread, a bunch of green bananas and once a watermelon, you don't know what happened to the rest of the money your mother gave him when you got here almost a month ago.

Earlier tonight, Big Daddy's hands were so shaky when he got the hot dogs out of the refrigerator, he dropped the package and the four remaining ones splattered onto the linoleum. Desmond took over, rinsed them off because they were covered in dirt and crumbs before placing them in the large pot filled with water. Big Daddy retreated to his chair in the corner of the living room, turned on the fan so it was blowing right on him and fell asleep. He slept while you and your brothers ate the hot dogs and the last of the potato chips, slept through you turning on the television and didn't wake up until the tattooed man arrived.

Bear accepts Desmond's explanation that Big Daddy has gone to the IGA and you watch a few more *Simpsons* episodes before getting ready for bed.

In the morning, you wake up first, like you always do. Because you're the girl and you turned twelve in June, Big Daddy said you should have the spare bedroom all to yourself and you didn't have to share it with your brothers like you did last summer. Instead, they're on the pull-out sofa bed in the living room. You walk past them, still asleep, the shades pulled all the way down, flapping against the window screens in the slight breeze.

Usually by this time in the morning, you'd find Big Daddy in the kitchen, already on his second cup of coffee, hunched over the *Daily Eagle*, doing the crossword at the yellow Formica table in the middle of the room. But he's not in here and the coffee maker is empty and unplugged. Some mornings, he brings his mug and the paper out to the screened-in porch which is just off the kitchen and settles into his favorite wicker chair, the one with green pillows and an ottoman. But he isn't out there either. You cross back through the living room to see if maybe he's still asleep. The door to his bedroom is open and you peer in, but his bed is made up just like it was yesterday. He isn't in the bathroom and his dentures aren't soaking in a glass of water by the sink like they usually are in the mornings. Maybe he's on a walk?

Except you have not seen your grandfather go on even one walk so far this summer. There is no new food in the refrigerator or the cupboards and nothing to indicate that he's been in the house at all since he went out last night with the tattooed man.

This isn't the first time he has left you and your brothers alone all night. Last week, when you got back from the lake, there was a note on the kitchen table explaining that he wouldn't be home until very late. "Don't wait up for me, xo your Big Daddy," the note ended. You didn't see him again until he came home the following morning and went straight to his bedroom and slept until dinner time. A couple of other nights, he went out after dinner instead of falling asleep in his easy chair and didn't come home until well past your bedtime.

Last summer, everything was different during the month you and your brothers stayed with Big Daddy. Your mom wasn't trying to get better so she could come get you every Friday and bring you back home with her for the weekend. Then she'd drive you back here early on Monday morning before turning around to work all week. You were at Big Daddy's only four nights at a time and sometimes your mom came and took you and your brothers home on Thursdays.

Last summer, there was always food and you didn't have to eat hot dogs every night for dinner. While you and your brothers went to the lake during the day, George Bachus, Big Daddy's best friend, came over and they spent the mornings watching game shows until the "girls" came by. Gladys and Janelle fixed lunch which they ate at the card table on the screened-in porch and they played canasta for the rest of the afternoon. You came home most days to find the four of them still going at it. Often, Big Daddy's friends stayed on well into the evening. Gladys and Janelle made dinner which they served on the screened-in porch and you all ate by candlelight. On some nights when they were in a particularly good mood, everyone pushed the furniture to the side and Big Daddy put on music they used to listen to when they were teenagers. He turned on the lamp with the red lightbulb and the room filled with a warm glow. Everyone danced, even Desmond, swinging from one set of arms to another, Big Daddy dipping you backwards when you got to him.

But this summer during the first week you were here, Desmond told you he thought Big Daddy was drinking again. Your grandfather used to show off his AA coins, boasted about going to meetings every, single Friday for ten years straight. It explained his shaky hands and the cloudy look in his eyes and why he gave you and your brothers drinks that resembled cocktails, juice and lemonade mixed with seltzer. Desmond said he saw Big Daddy slipping vodka into his drink as well as his cans of Fresca. George Bachus hasn't been over once the whole time you've been here and neither have Gladys or Janelle. Last summer, the next-door neighbors took you out on their motor boat a few times, dragging you behind on a large inflatable round disc with their grandsons. But now they're so mad at Big Daddy about something, they won't even say hello.

Staying at Big Daddy's this summer is not as much fun as last summer. But finally, it's the last week here and soon you'll be going home. Your mom is going to ask her boss for Friday off from work, she told you and Desmond on the phone over the weekend. All things being well, she'll pick you up Thursday evening. That means it could be just three more days you have to get through at Big Daddy's. She didn't need to tell you to keep it from Bear, in case her boss said no. Although he just turned nine and is the tallest boy in the entire third grade, still he's your baby Bear, will always be your baby Bear and you and Desmond are used to protecting him. He gets teased a lot because he's only friends with the girls and loves princess movies. It didn't help that he dressed up like Elsa for Halloween one year or wet himself in first grade after your dad moved away, which no one has ever forgotten. Some boys in Bear's class started calling him *Ed*, which is what they call the kids in the Special Ed classes. So Desmond hunted down the ring leader, telling him if he didn't leave Bear alone, there would be trouble, and that was the end of that.

But neither of you could do anything about Ron, your mom's ex-boyfriend, who taunted Bear, called him a sissy, a cry baby, made fun of him for watching *Little Mermaid* and *Frozen*, said those were "girl" movies. "What is wrong with you?" he always asked Bear. All you could do was comfort Bear when he cried and give Ron the dead-eye stare. Finally, your mom realized that Ron was a jerk and kicked him out. When he refused to leave, she put his things out on the street. He kept calling her and following her until she had to call the police. That was April. That's when you overheard your mom asking Big Daddy if he would take you and your brothers for all of July after school got out so she could "focus on getting better and feeling stronger."

Now you sit in Big Daddy's chair and wait for your brothers to wake up. The day before you left home and came out here, the three of you dyed your hair a mixture of gray and purple. Sometimes, you pretend to yourself that you are all in a band, like one of those family bands, called the Unaccompanied Minors, which is what they call you on the airplane when you go visit your dad and his new wife in Ohio. When your mom checks you in for the flight, you're given bright orange bracelets to wear so the flight attendants can identify you.

It's not even nine in the morning but already it's sweltering and you sweat and wait for your brothers to wake up, sweat and wait. Then you get your sketch pad and begin a drawing of them sleeping on the sofa bed, which is only a few feet away. You sketch the lumps of their bodies under the sheets, curled away from each other. Bear is turned toward you, his eyes fluttering slightly as he dreams. He sweats doing everything, including sleeping and his dirty hair is damp. You start to draw his face, adding a rivulet of perspiration that has formed along his hairline. Desmond is on the other side and he has the sheet pulled all the way over his head. You are working on drawing the television opposite the couch when your brothers wake up.

"Where's Big Daddy?" Bear asks. His purple and gray hair is sticking straight up.

"Big Daddy is out." You look at Desmond. You have a way of communicating with your older brother using only facial expressions.

"I want to call Mommy." Bear sticks out his lower lip.

"She's at work. We can't bother her," Desmond says.

"Why isn't Big Daddy back?"

"He's at that hardware store," Desmond says. "The one he likes in Lanesboro. Isn't that right, Nia?" Desmond looks at you and widens his eyes.

"Yeah, he went there." You nod slightly at Desmond, as if to say, *I'm on it.* "Come on, let's eat breakfast quick, okay Beary Bear. So we can get to the lake. It's so hot."

"We always go to the lake," Bear grumbles. "Can't we stay here today. Just once. And wait for Big Daddy to come back."

You and Desmond exchange another look.

"He's gonna be a while," Desmond says.

"Yeah and what are you talking about, silly? You love it at the lake." You jump onto the pull-out bed and start tickling him. Desmond joins in until Bear is giggling and pleading with you to stop and all three of you are laughing, as if it's like any other morning at Big Daddy's.

Breakfast is crumbs and dust from the boxes of Coco Pops and Froot Loops, the last of the cereal. The long-life milk is gone so you pour water into the bowls and spray Cool Whip on top of the gooey mixture until the can only squirts out air.

Usually after breakfast, back when there was still food, Bear would help you and Desmond make a picnic lunch to bring to the lake: peanut butter and banana sandwiches on Wonder bread wrapped in tin foil, a Tupperware container of grapes, bags of potato chips and water bottles which you would put in a cooler bag. This morning, you take three cans of Big Daddy's Fresca and a half bag of Doritos and head out. When you wheel your bikes past Big Daddy's car, you worry Bear will ask how he could have driven to the hardware store in Lanesboro without his car. You can tell Desmond is thinking of an explanation, but Bear doesn't seem to have noticed.

You peddle along Dalton Ave, take a right onto Alpine Road, following it until you reach Parking Area A. Highland Lake is long and seems to stretch on forever, well past the beach where you spend your days. People are always leaving behind water toys, inflatable flamingos, dolphins, rubber rings. Last week, you found a paddle board that had drifted onto the shore and didn't seem to belong to anyone. At the end of every day after that, you stashed it in the bushes so no one else would find it. It is still there in the same place as yesterday and Bear lies on top of it while you and Desmond push him out into the deep water, beyond where any of you can touch. You spin him around and then you swim over to the part of the beach with life guards and a roped-off swimming area with a raft that you dive off for a while. Then you drink the Frescas and eat the Doritos until the bag is empty and your fingertips have turned orange.

Big Daddy has been giving you money to get ice creams from the truck that arrives around midday. But today you have nothing when it pulls up, so you lie on your towels and watch as the other kids swarm it. A little boy drops his entire cone onto the sand. You long to run over, pick it up and eat it anyway. You can tell that Desmond and Bear are thinking the same thing.

At the beginning of the month, a group of families with a bunch of kids close in age to you and your brothers were at the beach every day and you folded in with them, playing together like you all had always known each other. The moms seemed to feel sorry for you and made sure to bring extra food for lunch every day for you and your brothers. They brought amazing hero sandwiches filled with salami and provolone and diced tomatoes and hots and lettuce, tuna salad with pickles and cheese and lettuce, black pepper turkey and Monterey Jack. They brought fried chicken and potato salad and watermelon slices and peaches and plums and strawberries from the local farm stands, giant-sized chocolate chip cookies for dessert. They fed you that whole entire week and let you be part of their large clan. And then, just like that, they were gone.

Another week, there was a boy around Desmond's age who was there with his mother and that boy joined in with your games. Yet another week, a group of girl cousins invited the three of you to play water tag and Marco Polo with them, and you had races with their boogie boards. The month has been passing by quickly enough. Until today.

You swim some more and then lie on your towels and nap before getting on your bikes and following the same route back to Big Daddy's cottage. When you get there, Big Daddy's car is parked in the same position in the driveway as when you left. The phone on the wall in the kitchen is ringing, but the person hangs up by the time you answer it, so you hear only dial tone. Big Daddy is not in the house.

The cottage sucks in heat all day long, so that by late afternoon every inch of it, both bedrooms, the kitchen, the screened-in porch, the living room and the tiny bathroom feel well over 100 degrees. You take a freezing cold shower and change into shorts and a sleeveless T-shirt. But a layer of sweat forms as soon as you sprawl out on the couch. Desmond drapes his legs on the other side and Bear takes his usual position on top of his sleeping bag on the floor. You watch *SpongeBob SquarePants*, *Family Feud*, and the local news. Dusk comes and still Big Daddy hasn't returned.

Bear starts to whine about being hungry. Even the hot dogs are gone, so you search the freezer, remembering a Tupperware container underneath the now long-gone ice cream. The blue cover is crusted into a block of ice and stuck to the wall so you and Desmond chip away at it until the container loosens. After running warm water over it, you pry the lid open to find something brown and defrost it in the microwave. Eventually it gets warm enough to eat, some kind of stew with potatoes and carrots and chunks of meat which resembles dog food, but you are all so hungry that you eat the whole thing, wiping the container clean with your fingertips.

Bear asks about calling your mom again, but Desmond says no.

"What about going over to Gladys' house," Bear suggests. "Remember when we went there last year? Before we went to the baseball game?"

You do remember and look over at Desmond. It's not a bad idea, you try to say to your older brother with your face. But Desmond says that you need to stay here, for when Big Daddy comes home.

"But what if Big Daddy doesn't come back tonight? What if he's in trouble?" Bear asks. You are thinking the exact same thing. He has never left you alone by yourselves for this long and it can only mean that something is very wrong.

"He's fine," Desmond says. "Go get ready for bed, okay?"

Bear's face crumples, but he listens, like he always does. He's used to obeying you and Desmond. It's your job to collect him from his classroom at dismissal every day. You bring him out to the yard where the little kids run around on the grassy area or chase each other in the school playground while parents and babysitters sit on the benches and talk to each other and the bigger kids shoot hoops into the basketball net. If it's raining, you take him to the library instead. Desmond goes to Mattison Regional, the 7-12 school, where you will go in the fall, and he meets you an hour later. You have to take a city bus and then there's another mile walk before you get home and your mom doesn't want you and Bear doing all that without Desmond.

On Tuesdays and Thursdays though, Desmond can't meet you because he has practice: soccer in the fall, basketball in the winter and track and field in the spring. Instead, you and Bear have to get a ride home with one of his classmates, Lucas, just because your mom and Lucas' mom are friends. Which would have been okay except for Lucas' older sister, Anna, who's in your grade.

Last winter, your mom had to start going to the food pantry at St. Michael's, which Anna found out about, because she makes everyone else's business her own. She came up to you one day at recess, with all of her stupid friends trailing behind her, holding a brown paper bag in her hand. Her friends were screeching like seagulls hovering above an overflowing garbage can.

"Anna don't," they cried after her. But she kept walking towards you with this funny look, like she might be suffocating, trying to swallow back laughter.

"Look at her, look!"

"She's doing it, she's doing it!"

"No, Anna!"

"Oh. My. God!"

You didn't understand what was happening until she was right in front of you. "Thought you might need this." Anna shoved the bag at you and skipped away.

"I can't believe it, I can't believe it, I can't believe it," her friends sang and ran after her. Inside the bag was a dented can of Spam with a St. Michael's Food Pantry brochure inside.

It only got worse after that. Anna corralled her friends to say under their breath, *St. Michael's* or *Ed's Sister,* whenever the teacher called on you. Then she told everyone that your mom was a slut, and got kids to whisper, *slut daughter,* whenever you passed them in the hallway. She made up a story about how your dad left and moved to Ohio because your mom slept around so much. He *had* to move to Ohio and then he became all religious, Anna told everyone. And everyone believed her lies. One day when Bear was going home with a friend, you fought her after school. A couple of her friends joined in and you got beat pretty bad. And it didn't stop them calling you names. In fact, it only made them do it more. And then every Tuesday and Thursday when Desmond was at practice, you had to sit in Anna's stupid mini-van with her and her mom and Lucas and Bear. You always made sure to ride in the way back and just stare out the windows, not saying anything to any of them. Her mom thought you were rude, but really, it was Anna. She's the one who is rude, not you.

Big Daddy is still not back when you wake up in the morning. There is one last bag of Jiffy Pop popcorn in the cupboard so you have that for breakfast when your brothers wake up. It's raining so you can't go to the lake. Instead you lie on the pull-out sofa bed and watch *Simpsons* reruns over and over and try to forget how hungry you are, but it's hard. There are so many commercials featuring food and even the ones about soup, which you hate, make you nauseous and dizzy with hunger.

It clears up in the afternoon so you bike out to the lake, but only because no one can stand being inside the cottage anymore. Desmond is irritable and storms off. Bear keeps getting upset over everything. He refuses to put on sunscreen and water gets up his nose. "I hate this stupid lake," he screams at you. "It's so boring. I hope I never have to come back here ever, ever again." Eventually, he wanders over to the beach and plays in the sand with a group of boys his age.

You lie on your towel, trying not to think about how hungry you are or where Big Daddy is or what has happened to him. Then you get out your sketch pad and start drawing Rufus, Big Daddy's emotional support dog who died right after Christmas. Big Daddy got Rufus years ago because of his PTSD. He's a veteran, like George Bachus, and suffers from nightmares and panic attacks. Sudden noise, like a car back firing or thunder, can make him agitated. But Rufus was specially trained to get behind Big Daddy to steady him whenever that happened to help him calm him. Now he's on the waiting list for another emotional support dog, but there are so many people with PTSD and not enough dogs so it will be a while, your mother explained when she told you and your brothers that Rufus was gone.

Last summer, you and your brothers used to go to the lake with Big Daddy in the early mornings before breakfast to walk Rufus. The lake would be quiet and still and sometimes smothered in fog. Off in the distance, you could see people fishing but the fog made them look not quite real, as if they were in a painting. Rufus liked chasing the ball into the water and you could throw it to him over and over again and he never got tired. You add a ball, a motorboat off in the distance and fog on the lake to your drawing.

Your brothers come and find you when the sun is low in the sky and you bike home. The cottage is empty when you get there and the only thing left to eat is a half box of stale Saltines. There is some relish and grape jelly and mayonnaise and an almost empty jar of Marshmallow Fluff that you and your brothers spread on top of the crackers. It helps dull the gnawing inside for a little while and you lie on the couch and turn on the television. Desmond sits in Big Daddy's chair and flips aimlessly up and down through all the channels, until Bear tells him to cut it out, cut it out. You are slick with sweat but you don't have enough energy to take a shower and you are so dizzy, you feel like you might fall over if you stand up.

"I'm so hungry," Bear starts to cry and Desmond tells him not to be such a baby.

"I'm scared." Bear gets up off his sleeping bag on the floor and curls up next to you on the couch. "What if he never comes back. What if we never see Big Daddy again. What if..."

"Shut up!" Desmond shouts. "Just stop talking okay? You're making everything worse."

"It already is worse. I want Mommy." He lies with his head in your lap and cries and you stroke his forehead. "Mommy, Mommy, Mommy," he whimpers, sniffing and wiping his face.

Last summer, the night you went to Gladys' house, you drove past the Lantern Bar and Grille and two men were fighting outside on the sidewalk. There was a crowd gathered round and you could hear the smacking sound that the men's fists made when they connected with each other's faces. One man got knocked to the ground and the other one was screaming while being held back by some of the bystanders. There was bright red blood coming from his nose and his mouth that spilled down onto his white T-shirt.

"Jesus, look at that bullshit," Big Daddy had said quietly. "I don't miss that, I really don't."

You wonder if that's where he went. Maybe he got a black eye there and doesn't want to come home until it goes away. The way you felt after Anna punched you so hard that the left side of your face was streaked red and swollen. You lied to your mom and Desmond, told them it had happened during gym when a basketball hit your face. You didn't want your older brother saying anything to Anna because it wouldn't have helped. You faked a stomachache for two days straight so you could stay home until your face healed and no one could see what Anna had done to you.

The three of you fall asleep in the living room with the television on, first Bear atop of his sleeping bag on the floor, then Desmond starts snoring slightly, his head tilted back, and eventually you must have as well because when you open your eyes again, the room is filled with mid-morning light. The television is still on. Your neck twinges from sleeping at a weird angle on the arm of the couch. You look around one last time, even though you already know that Big Daddy is not in the house.

You go in the kitchen and pull the long phone cord out to the screened-in porch and call your mother, even though Desmond has kept saying that you shouldn't. You need to know when exactly you are going home.

"Hey baby," she says and the sound of her voice makes you well up.

"How are you feeling, Mommy? Did you get Friday off?"

"I'm feeling so much better, baby. And Sheila said I could take Friday as a vacation day. Yeah! So I can come pick you guys up tomorrow. I can't wait. I need to see my babies. Oh I miss you guys so much."

"I miss you too, Mommy." Tears start streaming down your face and you cry quietly, hoping she doesn't notice.

"Have you been having fun at the lake this week? You guys are so lucky to be out there right now, this heat is unbelievable. I need to get going though, okay baby? I gotta get to work. I'll call you guys later. And tomorrow, I'll drive out as soon as I finish work, so I should be there around 6. I can't wait."

"I can't either, Mommy."

You hang up the phone and check to see if your brothers have woken, but Desmond is still sprawled out in Big Daddy's chair, and Bear is on the floor, both still asleep. You are too excited to sit down. You pace back and forth between the kitchen, the screened-in porch, the living room and back again, trying to resist the urge to wake your brothers and tell them the good news. You are going home. You will eat again. Soon.

You go into Big Daddy's room and sit on his bed. Sometimes in the middle of the night, you wake to the sound of him crying out for help. Your mom said when she was little and Big Daddy was still drinking, he once got so angry that he hit your gran. You don't remember her, but there's a photograph in your kitchen back home of your grandmother holding your head in the palm of her hand when you are only a few weeks old.

You go over to Big Daddy's bureau to look at the framed pictures he has on top of it. There is one that was taken four years ago of you and your brothers with both your parents standing in front of your Christmas tree. Before your father left.

Desmond has been angry with your father ever since he moved to Ohio. You have a baby brother there, or at least your father says he is your brother. But he's not your brother in the way that Desmond and Bear are. You've met him twice since he was born last year. The first time was at Thanksgiving when Desmond refused to hold him and your father said if he was going to be like that, he wasn't welcome in their home any more. But his new wife, Lisa, took your father into the kitchen and talked to him in a soft voice. When he came back into the living room and told Desmond he was sorry, so sorry, he really looked it. He even cried a little and hugged

Desmond, holding onto him for a long time until your brother hugged him back.

You like holding your baby brother, even though he will never be your real brother. And at first, you tried not to like Lisa. But she is really nice, and not in a fake way where she lets you do whatever you want when you go visit her and your father. She always talks to your mom, before you go, to find out what you and your brothers like to eat and do, what your mother's rules are, bedtimes, things like that, to be sure they do everything the same way.

Although Ron was the worst, most of your mom's other boyfriends have been pretty awful. They treat you and your brothers as if you're the most badly-behaved kids they've ever met. Even though you all have good manners and help out at home. Even though your mom always says how lucky she is, that you are the best kids, the best thing that ever happened to her.

Behind the photograph, you notice a jam jar full of change in the far corner of Big Daddy's bureau. You tip it onto the floor and sort the coins into piles of pennies, nickels, dimes and quarters. You make rows on the rug and start to count. It's eleven dollars and 43 cents. You rush into the living room to wake up your brothers.

Everyone is giddy as you get on your bikes and start off for the McDonald's on Route 7. You went once at the beginning of the month and it's only a few minutes away by car. But it takes much longer by bike and you have to go up a steep hill and the sun radiates off the asphalt as if you are pedaling inside a pizza oven. You take a right onto Route 7, the truck route through town, which doesn't have a bike lane. 18-wheelers and tractor trailers keep speeding past you. You look back from time to time to make sure Bear hasn't been run over. Finally, you round a corner and there it is, just up ahead.

Ten minutes later, the three of you sit on the curb in the parking lot with cheeseburgers and French fries and Cokes spread out before you. You're so hungry, you can hardly wait to put the ketchup on. It's an incredible feeling to eat real food again with your brothers, their purple and gray hair, damp with sweat, glistening in the hot July sunshine.

Sometimes when you're at the lake, you pretend to yourself that you and your brothers are famous and everyone on the beach knows it, all the moms with their kids and babies, the baby sitters, the campers wearing the same T-shirts, the life guards, the people walking their dogs, the groups of families, the kayakers, the water-skiers, the people fishing on outboard motor boats, all of them are staring at you, admiring you. Later, they will tell their friends, their families, guess who we saw at the lake? Yeah, that's right. We saw that band and it was definitely them. They were there all right, they were totally there.

We Own the Jetty

by Catherine Elcik

So, my friend Dario gets fired from Burger King for salting the same batch
of fries nine times. Dario tells me when his manager canned him, he was
holding the shaker in his hand, ready to do it again. Now I can see how
it might have looked like Dario was playing a prank, but D's one of those
guys who can't leave for work before he makes damn sure his apartment's
all locked up — his record's five trips between his car and his front door.
Most of the time Dario has his repeat-repeat thing under control, but it
always gets worse when he's stressed. Ike was shot in a Store24 two nights
ago. That's more than enough to wind Dario up.

Ike was a bit younger than the rest of us; he would have turned
twenty-one a couple months after he was killed. Me, Dario, and Pudge had
big plans for that birthday — a Sox game at Yankee stadium, then a strip
club in Jersey where Dario's cousin swore you could buy skin on skin in the
Champagne room. The tickets have been wedged under the molding by my
phone for weeks. It was supposed to be a surprise. The morning of Ike's
funeral, I wear a dark suitcoat and a tie over my blackest jeans. I grab a few
nip bottles from the kitchen. When I see the tickets on the wall, I take them
too.

Outside the church, Dario, Pudge, and me wait for Ike's girl,
Shawna, on the corner. I offer up my cigarettes and Dario takes one; Pudge
waves me away. Since leaving East Boston, Pudge got taller and thinner
than any of the rest of us, but no one's gonna stop calling him Pudge; not
after all this time. We're looking down the street for Shawna. Dario fidgets.
Pudge shoves his hands into his pockets. I offer them booze — two chugs
and it's gone. We don't talk.

I see Shawna first. She's drooped against her sister's arm, staring
at the sidewalk; I've seen her looking better on days she was hungover

and curled around a toilet. I toss my bottle into the bushes in front of the rectory and wave — just two fingers in the air. I know she sees me because she snaps her head up for a second before letting it tilt back to one side. She starts to shake. I walk toward her. Dario and Pudge follow me. We circle her. She leans on me. We enter the church as a crowd.

***

Ike and I met when we were thirteen-year-old fosters at Regents Hall for Boys in East Boston. When he died, I'd known Ike for eight years — that's two more than I got with my birth mom. Ike had a thing for underdogs; he pulled Dario in with us first, then Pudge. He tried to get Dario and me to quit using Pudge as a nickname — "the kid's name is Paolo," he'd say — which was rich considering it was Ike who got people to call me Frankie instead of Francis, but Ike said there was no comparison. My name stopped beatings where Pudge's name baited them, so we kept his nickname among us after that, but Pudge didn't seem to mind. He was a smart guy, the kind of kid who pulled off straight-As in his sleep — Pudge made sure none of us failed algebra; we made sure no one at Regents beat him up.

It was Ike who figured out that the night monitors didn't pay any attention to the entrance by the kitchen, but once we were outside there were nothing but shitty East Boston triple-deckers for blocks in every direction. I said we should hop the train to Revere Beach, but Dario, who was already nervously collecting all the litter he saw on the sidewalk, reminded us there was a state police barracks right on the water. "You never know which cops will ignore you and which ones'll turn you in," he said as he picked up a Dunkin' Donuts cup and shoved it into his pocket.

Going to Winthrop was Pudge's idea — he'd been with a foster family out on Point Shirley once and swore Winthrop at night was just a beach and a bunch of sleepy houses. Plus, there was this liquor store near the Orient Heights T stop that didn't ask for ID if you paid cash — because I looked the oldest, Ike sent me in to make the purchase, but I came out with a fifth of Jack.

"We said beer," Ike said, but I shrugged.

"Can't hide a twelve-pack in my shirt."

We took the 712 bus past the *Welcome to Winthrop* sign, houses with driveways, and a mess of convenience stores. Then the driver turned the last corner and it was nothing but ocean. Pudge signaled for the bus to stop and we walked down the hill toward the water on a street so empty, so quiet, so boring, I was ready to take my chances in Revere — screw the state police.

"What do we do now?" I asked.

"We gotta walk like we belong here," Pudge muttered as we approached a man leading a retriever on a leash. Pudge waved at him, and the man smiled. Once the street was empty again, the four of us darted through an opening in the sea wall and scrambled down the stairs to a rock beach between two jetties.

I pulled out that bottle of Jack.

"Are you nuts?" Dario hissed. "They catch us with that they'll send us somewhere worse than Regents."

"The wall's too high, jackass," Ike said. "We might as well be invisible."

Ike called these trips to Winthrop "taking the jetty." Every Saturday we could scrounge up enough cash to cover the train and bus rides, we went. One night I stood up on the sea wall shaking a can of black spray paint.

"Put that away!" Dario paced as he fastened and unfastened the strap of his digital watch. "You're gonna get us all arrested."

The street was empty, and I laughed. "By *who?*"

I popped the cap off and sprayed *WE OWN THE JETTY* onto the concrete in giant, crooked letters. The four of us stood back to admire my work. Ike slapped me on the back.

"Yeah," he said. "*Fuck* yeah."

***

After the funeral, we sit at the bar in *The Eastie* waiting for the beer to kick in. After each sip, Dario wipes his bottle, then smoothes the wrinkles in his napkin before lining it up with the edge of the table. Pudge checks his watch; his flight to California leaves in a couple hours. Shawna stares at the television. Nobody's saying much so, I ask Pudge about Stanford.

"You still farting around with those philosophy classes?" I ask.

Pudge sips his beer. "*Psychology.*"

"At least he's doing something." Dario straightens his napkin and lines it up with the edge of the table. "Which is more than you can say."

I slap the Red Sox tickets on the table. Pudge picks one up and turns it over in his hand. Dario stares at his beer.

"Ike always wanted to see a game at Yankee Stadium, so I say we still go," I tell them. "The three of us. Shawna too, if she wants."

Shawna looks at us then turns back to the television. "You know I can't." She has some wedding or family reunion to go to that weekend. Ike was supposed to go with her, but it was the same weekend the Sox were playing in New York. I've never heard anyone yell as loud as Shawna did the day she found out I'd bought tickets for the one weekend she'd told me to avoid.

Dario straightens the remaining tickets into a pile. He looks at me and runs a hand through his hair three times fast.

Pudge empties his beer and glances at his watch. "I don't know, Frankie."

"What do you mean you don't know? That funeral was bullshit." I point to the tickets. "*This* is the sendoff Ike would have wanted."

Pudge drops the ticket back onto the pile. "It just doesn't seem right."

"I don't believe what I'm hearing." I slam my beer against the table. "If Ike were here, no way he'd let any of us back out. Us three, the Sox, Yankee Stadium — Ike'll haunt us if we *don't* go. Are you in or are you in?"

Dario shrugs. "I'm in, I guess."

Pudge glances at his watch and stands up to put on his coat.

"What about you?" I ask.

"I've got a plane to catch and finals to study for — you can understand that, right?" He holds his hand out to me, but I don't shake it.

He hugs Dario, kisses Shawna on the cheek, and then he's gone. It pisses me off that he's weaseling out of the game, but Shawna points out he's already dropped everything once to be at the funeral at all. I'd have rather he skipped the funeral and come to the game, but Shawna says I gotta let Pudge be Pudge, that he's just saying goodbye the best way he knows how, that we all are.

Shawna knocks back another shot.

Dario lines the napkin up with the edge of the table for the hundredth time.

I wave the tickets between Dario and me — "Looks like it's just us, man" — and slip them back into my pocket.

***

Shawna went to East Boston High with the rest of us. Back then, she had short hair dyed black, and she wore necklaces made of bike chains. The summer before we were in tenth grade, Ike had it bad.

"You're wasting your time, man," Dario said. "Shawna eats muff."

Ike grabbed the bottle of Jack out of Dario's hands. "Don't be a jackass."

Dario had to tell himself Shawna was gay so he could feel better about the way she shot him down at the beginning of the school year. The thing about Shawna was, if you could get beyond all the black clothes and freak jewelry, she had this nose that came to a perfect point, these big fleshy lips, and her eyes just bore into you — one blue, the other kind of green.

When Ike first started bringing Shawna to the jetty, she was just another one of the guys — she shared cigarettes, she laughed, she spit —

but once she and Ike had been going out long enough for them to stand with their hands in the butt pocket of each other's blue jeans, she changed. Suddenly, anytime one of us told a joke about some girl from school, Shawna rolled her eyes and told us we were pig fuckers. Then there was the sex thing. Whenever Shawna was at the beach, she convinced Ike to disappear with her to the far side of the jetty. We never saw anything, but when the waves weren't crashing in hard, we heard plenty. It didn't bother me much, but it drove Dario crazy.

After a few months Dario started climbing the jetty to watch Shawna and Ike go at it. Might have got away with it if he hadn't insisted on opening and closing the Velcro strap on his watch as he crouched there.

All I could hear was Shawna's scream and Ike shouting. Then I saw Ike up on the jetty beating on Dario. If they talked about that night at all, I never heard them. Dario spent the next couple of weeks with a black eye, and Shawna and Ike stopped doing it while we were around. By the time Dario's bruise healed, he and Ike seemed like they were back to normal.

***

After Pudge leaves the bar to catch his plane the night of the funeral, Shawna, Dario and me do a tour of East Boston's finest. By the time we're done, it's late, and Shawna's the only one sober enough to drive. She drops Dario off first, then pulls up in front of my house.

"Ike was a stupid fuck," she says. "You guys make out like he was this God. Gods don't die at Store24."

"Nobody really knows what happened that night," I tell her.

"The fuck we don't."

I look away. In the security tapes they'd played on the news, Ike's at the counter paying for cigarettes when a guy in a kid-size Big Bird mask comes in with a gun, points it at the camera, and fires. When the police find them, Ike and the clerk are slumped in a corner with bullets in their brains, the cash register's empty, and there isn't a carton of cigarettes left

in the store. The way I figure it, Ike went hero and reached for the gun.
Good-bye brain. Goodbye Ike from Maverick Square.

"Ike was a stupid fuck," Shawna says again, hands on the wheel,
head down. Her hair's long and brown now — no more black dye; no
more hard jewelry. Just a normal girl crying over a dead boy.

Outside, a group of teens laugh as they walk past the car.

I try changing the subject, but my voice sounds fake even to me.
"At least Dario's gonna go to Yankee Stadium like we planned."

"Whatever." Shawna cracks her window and flicks her cigarette to
the curb, but then she's on me — her tongue in my mouth, a hand on my
crotch.

I go with it a second, before I push her away. "Jesus, Shawna."

She slumps against the driver's seat. "You too drunk?"

"Ike was like a brother."

"Ike's dead."

"*Barely.*"

I scramble out of her car.

***

A week after Ike's funeral, Shawna calls to tell me something's not right
with Dario. She brought him a lasagna and he put it in the dishwasher.
Now he's not answering his phone. Could I go and check it out? Dario's
meds normally cut through his neat-freak bullshit, but sometimes, when
the world gets fucked enough, Dario's record skips until someone nudges
the needle to get him back on track. Ike and I saw it happen a few times; the
worst was when Dario's birth-dad died. He framed the one photo he had
of him and his father and was hellbent on finding the best spot to hang it.
When we got to him, there were a hundred nails in the wall, and Dario's
thumb was bleeding where he'd missed and hit himself with the hammer.
Ike and me took the photo and left him with a bottle of Jack.

Tonight, though, Dario's cleaning. I smell the bleach in the hall outside his apartment; inside, the reek makes my eyes burn. I open the window in Dario's living room, then walk toward the back of his apartment. His bathroom is a nightmare of gleaming chrome. In the kitchen, Dario's on his hands and knees pouring bleach directly onto the tiles. He puts the Clorox down, picks up a brush with bent bristles, and scrubs so hard his body bobs in time with his arm. He's coughing. He could kill us both with a few drops of ammonia.

"D," I say.

Dario keeps scraping the floor. His hands are red and chapped, and the knees of his jeans are soaked through.

"Hey," I try again.

"The fucker won't come clean." His face nearly touches the tile.

If Ike were here, he'd tackle Dario, but that's not my style. I snatch the bottle of bleach while Dario's attention's on the floor. I'm halfway down the hall before he yells after me. I jump into the bathroom and ignore Dario banging on the locked door as I pour and flush. When I hand him the empty bottle, Dario sucker-punches me and storms off. I stumble after him. In the kitchen Dario raids the cabinet under the sink. Comet and Fantastic crash to the floor, then Dario holds up the Windex. When he puts a finger on the trigger, I knock the bottle out of his hand.

"You want to kill us both?" I scream at him. "What would that prove, huh? What the hell would that prove?"

Once Dario's calm, we open windows and take two beers up to the roof. The smell of bleach clings to our clothes and hair as we watch the mid-day arrivals scream into the airport — United, American, some puddle jumper.

"You OK?" I ask.

Dario wipes his beer on his shirt. "I think I'm over the worst of it, and then it just hits me, you know?"

"You gotta pull it together," I say.

"Fuck off." Dario turns his beer around three times in his hand. Each time he moves I smell chlorine on his sleeve.

✳✳✳

I didn't realize how many people in Winthrop ordered Chinese food until
Ike died and I noticed I passed the jetty with greasy take-out piled on my
passenger seat sometimes as many as six times a night. I won't go out there,
of course — I haven't in years — but sometimes I pull over and take it all
in.

The lights on the planes hover way out over the water before
slowly inching forward, their jets growling as they swoop over the beach in
their descent to the airport on the other side of the harbor. My eyes drift to
the rocks that make up the jetty.

Most of the time the four of us spent out here we were just
shooting the shit, but once in a while Pudge got us talking about the
dreams we usually kept to ourselves — Ike wanted to be a detective, Dario
wanted to open a pub called *Dario's Den*, and I wanted to be a pilot.

"Not that it matters," I told Pudge.

Pudge's face went red. "You act like we're all stuck here forever."

Pudge didn't mean to be a clueless son of a bitch — he honestly
saw it as a simple equation: work for what you want and you get it. Which
was fine for a guy with a brain like his, but what was I gonna do? Waltz
into the airport and ask where to sign up? Pudge might go off and do the
school thing one day, but the rest of us would never be much more than the
rejects we were back then.

These days I want to own a house way more than I ever wanted
to fly. I stare at the tip of Point Shirley, a spit of land that juts out from
the rest of Winthrop. This is the part of town that's directly under Logan
Airport's flight path. The people who live there are used to the planes
gunning over their crouching houses and the rumble they feel as the jet
engines scream overhead. Houses out here are pretty cheap — I guess
you pay less when you sign up for a better-than-average chance of waking
up with a cockpit in the middle of your living room. Whenever I have a
little money left over at the end of the week, I tell myself this is what I'm

saving for — a cottage out here at the end of the world. But the last time I checked fifteen hundred bucks doesn't buy much of a house.

***

A few weeks later, a delivery takes me by Dario's and I decide to stop in — partly to check on him, partly to remind him about the Yankees game the following month — and find Shawna inside, which is weird. What's weirder is they've just finished dinner. Weirder still, they act super casual and welcome me, offer me a plate — there are leftover fajitas and there'll be hot brownies any second — but my stomach sours at the scent of roasted chicken mingled with chocolate.

In the kitchen there's a picked over plate of chicken and peppers on the table. The salsa spilled on the floor is bright red against the white tile. There's a dirty skillet in the sink. A mixing bowl smeared with chocolate.

On the counter, a timer ticks down a final thirty seconds.

Shawna squints through the oven window.

Dario pulls down three plates. He lines them up in a neat row, then stacks them, then lines them up again.

Shawna glances at me as she pulls on an oven mitt.

Dario keeps fidgeting with the plates, stacking them, lining them.

"They're just plates, man," I tell him. "Let it go."

Dario frowns and turns to the sink. Flips the faucet on full blast.

Shawna pulls the brownies from the oven and sets them on the stove.

Dario scrubs the pans, water pissing everything.

"Hey, we talked about this," Shawna coos at him.

"Yeah, cut the shit man," I try.

The steel wool hisses as Dario scrubs all the harder.

I'm about three seconds from yanking that brush out of Dario's hand when Shawna sidles to his side and closes her hand over his.

Dario goes still, but the faucet continues full blast.

My throat goes dry.

Shawna flips the faucet off but doesn't let go of Dario's hand.

When he leans against Shawna, it knocks the wind out of me.

***

We lost the jetty the night Ike turned seventeen. The big one-seven wasn't much to celebrate at Regents — it meant we only had one year until they kicked our asses to the curb; Regents may have still been the same shithole it was when we all got there, but it was the first real home any of us knew, so we weren't in any rush to leave it. Ike was drinking heavily — the bottle of Jack I'd scored for his birthday was half empty before the rest of us had more than a few sips.

"Here's to one more year as a reject," Ike said. Then he tipped back another long drink. Normally Shawna kept him from getting so trashed, but her shift didn't end for a few hours.

We didn't see the punks until they were on us. Their voices were deeper than ours; their stubble was thick. They smelled so sour, they had to have been at least as drunk as Ike. The shortest guy, the one they called Sal, stood slightly in front of the two skinny guys he was with. Even in the moonlight I could tell he was all muscle.

"Are you the shits who *own* the jetty?" Sal asked.

Ike staggered forward. "Depends on the shits asking."

I stepped between Ike and Sal. "It's his birthday, man. Give him a break."

"I don't care if it's Christmas Eve," Sal said.

Sal grabbed the Jack from Ike and drank. Ike swiped at the bottle, but he lost his footing and sat down hard on the jetty. He struggled to stand back up.

The men laughed, and I stepped forward. "That doesn't belong to you."

Sal took another long swig, then passed the bottle to the guy on his right. I stood up straighter. I stared him down. I could sense Dario and Ike just behind me. I held my hand out for the bottle. Pudge stood about a foot behind us all.

"We don't want any trouble," I said, and Sal laughed.

"Then why are you still here?"

In a low voice, Pudge tried to convince Dario, Ike, and me to bail. When we ignored him, he backed away a few feet. Then he turned, ran across the beach, and scrambled up the rocks to the stairs in the sea wall.

Sal took another drink. "Me and my friends are going down to the end of the jetty to finish this bottle — you want to be gone by the time we're done." Sal pushed between me and Dario; the other two went around Ike. We stared at them as they settled in to drink our booze on our jetty.

Dario picked up four rocks and arranged them into a straight line, then into a square, then back into a line, the rocks tapping together with a metallic click.

"We better go find Pudge," he said, and Ike climbed down from the jetty.

I jumped after him, got right up in his face. "So that's it?" I yelled. "We're just gonna take it?"

Ike kicked at the shells and rocks at his feet.

The water lapped against our sneakers.

Dario's rocks clicked and clicked and clicked.

"Fuck that." Ike took a stone from Dario's hand.

At the end of the jetty, Sal and his friends laughed in low voices.

Ike chucked the rock and hit the side of Sal's neck; if Ike had been sober, he might have beaned Sal and killed him.

Sal grabbed his throat and dropped the bottle — the sound of glass smashing is the last thing I remember before they were on us.

***

Shawna doesn't look me in the eye as she hands me a plate, and I know my suspicions are right. In the living room a few minutes later, Dario takes Shawna's hand and tells me what I already know.

I choke down that brownie and swear I'm happy for them.

Shawna doesn't say much — probably worried I don't know enough to keep my mouth shut about the way she threw herself at me the night of the funeral — but Dario says plenty.

That the two of them were building something real.

That he'd never felt stronger.

That he'd decided to be Shawna's plus one at her cousin's wedding.

I blink. "The wedding that's the same day as Ike's Yankee's game?"

"Yeah, do you mind?"

"Does it matter?"

"That trip's a bad idea, Frankie, you know?" Dario glances quickly at Shawna. "The truth is when she asked me to go with her, I felt like I'd been sprung from jail."

"From *jail?*"

"You know what I mean," Dario says. "I was relieved."

They look at each other then — just for a second — but it's as final as the three thousand miles Pudge put between him and the rest of us.

As final as Ike's grave.

***

After the glass shattered that day on the jetty, Ike went down fast and stayed there. One of the tall fucks got me in the eye — when I fell to my knees, he stepped onto my back and flattened me against the beach. The shells and rocks tore into my face. He wrung my left arm back further than any arm was ever meant to stretch — after a pop and a fuck-load of pain, it stretched back even more.

Beside me Dario whimpered then screamed, and I was sure we were dead men — all of us — until Pudge returned with flashing lights and EMTs.

Sal and the rest of them broke something in all of us — my arm snapped, Ike's skull was fractured, Dario's rib punched through his lung.

In time, we all healed, but we never returned to that jetty.

None of us did.

Not even me.

Not until today, the day I was supposed to be at a Yankee's game with Dario and Pudge and Ike.

Today, I walk out to the jetty alone.

Shells crunch underfoot as I get close.

My foot slips as I climb the rocks.

The waves crest and crash beneath me.

I pull the tickets out of my pocket and hold them in the breeze.

I know things haven't been the same since Ike and Dario and Pudge and me left Regents, but I always figured we were like the tide — high, then low, then back to high. I never guessed we might be shells tossed together by an ocean that could just pick us up and scatter us again.

Above me, a plane screams as it begins its descent, and I tear the tickets into a dozen tiny pieces.

I hold them so tight my hand throbs.

My heart races.

I watch the plane bear down, a sixteen wheeler with wings, until it drops out of sight to land safely on a tarmac I can't see.

Then — breathing deep the stink of the tide — I toss the tickets into the wind and, as the pieces flutter down to the rocks, to the sea, I turn and walk away.

Karaoke in the Lounge
of the Gods

by Paul H. Curtis

"In its encounter with the core of Israelite faith, the Canaanite cosmos was emptied of divinity; the heavens, until now studded with gods, became the handiwork of YHWH; the gods died; living myth became poetic metaphor and decorative motifs; forms were filled with new content. So we are told by many scholars."

    – Chaim Potok, *Wanderings*

YHWH stands in the congregation of the mighty, rendering his judgment among the gods.

"How long," he asks them, "will you defend the wicked? You should side with the weak and the fatherless. You should take up the cause of the poor and the oppressed. You know nothing; you walk about in darkness and the foundations of the earth are shaken. Once I called you gods: immortal children of the Most High. But you will perish like men."

"Listen," says Baal Haddad. "We're trying our best."

At last YHWH storms from the hall, and the thunder follows. For three thousand years the Elohim sit in silence, and then it is Enki who speaks.

"Well," he says, "that was awkward." Enki, lord who rides the storm, lion of heaven, looks down at his fingernails. The others wait for him to speak again, but he does not. Mighty waters flow upon his shoulders; an eagle perches at his arm. He smiles apologetically.

Enki's reticence troubles Baal Haddad. How have they come to this? Tongues tied, every one of them. He ought to drown the world in his wrath, but his wrath will not come. "I guess we'll talk about this at the next meeting," he says, though it is clear to him already that there will be no more meetings of the Elohim.

Anat drives him home. "I'll put a boot up his ass," she says. "I'll bathe in his blood."

"Watch the light," says Baal Haddad.

"I mean, who does he think he is?"

"The light."

They clear the intersection late; a red-light camera flashes behind them.

"Oh wait," says Anat, sarcastically: "I mean, who does He think He is?"

"He is who he is," says Baal Haddad.

"He wants to talk about the fatherless. As if we had never known what it is to lose the favor of a father. And the *oppressed.* But look how they multiply, on *his* watch!" Droplets fly from her glossed lips. The tendons in her neck are taut.

Baal Haddad loves his sister with a ferocity equaled only by the force of her own temper. But he is tired, and there is a tension at the base of his skull and behind his eyes; already he knows that he is in for three days of miserable headaches. He presses his fingertips against his brow; he does not respond.

The car swerves as Anat gestures. "I'll cut off his head and wear it as a jewel," she says.

"Anat —"

"But You," she says, turning to face Baal Haddad. "What are *You* going to do about it?"

He sighs. "What do you want me to do about it?"

"Passive," she spits, and she turns her eyes to the road again, just soon enough to avoid colliding with the median. "Apathetic. Letting him steal your thunder."

"I'm not saying —"

"*You,* who vanquished Yam and took his body to pieces, You the very conqueror of Death —"

"Anat," says Baal Haddad. "I'm not in the mood for a pep talk."

She leaves him at the bottom of the hill. Baal Haddad slouches up the steps toward his house. Its great cedar timbers no longer inspire him; all he can think about is what a bitch the place is to winterize. Especially the windows, which he thundered into being without considering the kind of maintenance they would require. You make a lot of mistakes with your first house, thinks Baal Haddad. But it's one thing to understand the mistakes. It's another thing having to live with them.

Shala is in the kitchen, baking. Her tablet is propped on the counter in front of her, and she is speaking to it. As Baal Haddad passes, she smiles at him — kindly, but so quickly that few of her viewers will notice. Her clever fingers go on weaving strips of dough.

In the bedroom, Baal Haddad removes his shoes and his great horned headdress and spreads himself atop the duvet. The bed, in a pool of moonlight by the windows of the big dark room, is bright and fresh; the pillows are scented with lavender. He regrets the fact that the blinds are open, but he does not move to close them. He closes his eyes instead. Is this what it feels like? he wonders. Is this how it begins? Perhaps after all he really is susceptible to the kind of emotional oblivion he has seen in others — something he has long feared, but never quite believed. He has always been a moody god, but until now his moods have ranged across the full spectrum: sullenness and despair, yes, but also ecstasy, also passion, also joy. And wrath, of course. Vigorous, righteous anger. Once again he tries to summon it, but still his wrath does not come. Probably this is for the better. Anger, so admirable in youth, does not become the elderly. Of course he is not yet so aged, but what comfort is that? He has reached a strange juncture in his existence: no longer a god, nor yet an old man. Just Haddad, on a bed, feeling nothing.

***

At the end of the street, Anat does not turn right, toward home. Instead she turns left, onto a long strip of divided highway flanked by gas stations and fast-food restaurants and half-lit strip malls and discount stores. She slides a Dead Kennedys CD into her aging hatchback's audio system, turns up the volume, cracks the window, lights a cigarette, and picks up a ragged Nietzsche paperback, which she holds against the steering wheel with her right hand while she smokes with her left, periodically tipping ashes into the cold stream of air and glancing every so often from the page to the road. She lets her foot fall heavily on the gas, easing up at intersections to time the traffic signals. Alternating bands of light and shadow drift across her as she drives.

There is an acid feeling in her stomach, not from hunger or indigestion, but from the always-loathsome exercise of bucking her brother up with false credit for deeds which were really her own. It was she, after all, who slew Death and fed his entrails to the birds, while Haddad was sulking in the underworld. And could Haddad have vanquished Yam without her? Without her, would he have that magnificent house upon the hill? No, and no again. But if her brother is nothing without her, the fact of her station within the patriarchy of the gods is that neither can she, for all her might, rule without him. And anyway she loves him — she really does, and it kills her to see him like this.

The value of a thing, she reads, *sometimes does not lie in that which one attains by it, but in what one pays for it.*

Fuuuuck, she thinks. Fucking Nietzsche. I could have told him that.

Now that she thinks of it, she's sure she *did* tell him that. For all the whispering she did into the old bastard's ear, he ought to have paid her royalties.

None of them understand this. Degenerate lazy leftover gods: if they'd ever paid the slightest attention they might have noticed that the source of her strength — the strength with which she has propped up their whole rotting dynasty — is the very price she has paid for exercising it. The paradox of her divinity, lacking the entitlement of masculinity, is how it grows in the gap between their dependence upon her and the respect they owe her. But there's no point in trying to explain it to them — she's seen enough blank gazes to last an eternity.

The CD skips and she pounds the player with a fist. She tosses the spent cigarette out the window and lights another.

Even the few who understand that she has paid a price do not understand the price she's paid. Shala pities her, for example, because Shala abhors the thought of Anat's empty apartment, her solo nights out at the bars, her perpetual partnerlessness; Shala thinks it must be lonely to love one's brother and no one else — and no doubt there's a touch of jealousy in her feelings about the bond between her husband and Anat, but Shala is a creature of such kindness and sympathy that the jealousy must be buried somewhere deep: down wherever it is she buries the truth about her marriage to Haddad, which is that it's only a footnote to the story of a mighty god whose sister is the source of his might. Shala, sweet goddess of the grains, does not understand that for Anat the price is the power, and the power is the price, nor can she see how the apathy of the Elohim threatens to make it all — the power and the sacrifices alike — worth nothing. Maybe I'm the only one left with anything to lose, Anat thinks.

War trumpets sounding in her veins, Anat cuts off an SUV in the center lane, hoping to provoke a road rage incident. But the SUV yields without returning her challenge.

The arrogance of YHWH, claiming sole representation of the eternal!

She's too angry now to keep this all in her head. Squeezing the cigarette between two fingers, she picks up her phone and selects a number from the contacts, the Nietzsche book still propped against the wheel, the old hatchback making fifteen over the limit down a dark stretch of highway out past the mall. The phone rings six times and dumps her into voicemail.

"It's Anat," she says. "Listen. This fucking Tetragram motherfucker needs to stay in his lane. I need to know why you didn't say anything back there. Like, are you even mad about this? Motherfucker's trying to *son* you. He's trying to be the whole band. I mean, how can there be only one avatar of the Almighty? What a piss-poor universe that would be! One mind, one personality, one stupid...*face*. You know what: you should have listened; you should have perked up those big ugly ears — I told you this — you should have paid attention when he said his people were talking about monotheism. Like, I know you don't do big words, big guy, but that should have caught your attention. I *told* you. *Mono*, motherfucker. Means *one*. What did you think was gonna happen? I told Haddad; I said to him, *Nip this shit in the bud.* But he's been moping around like —"

Here the voicemail app cuts her off.

She throws the cigarette out the window and lights another. She calls again; again she is sent to voicemail.

"And you know what? Let's get honest about who's been holding it all together. The motherfucking *war goddess* has been holding it all together. Did fucking Tetragram slay the serpent with the seven heads? Did YHWH get rid of the Quarrelsome One, or Zabib, or Ishat the Bitch of the Gods? No. *I* did. The motherfucking *war goddess* did. So if y'all don't want to do your jobs anymore, maybe you can at least have my fucking back for once so I can straighten this shit out."

She ends the call, and calls once again, and once again she is greeted by the voicemail.

"I know you're there," she says. "Pick up, you coward."

Giving up at last, she drops the phone and the book onto the passenger seat, turns off the stereo, and drives hard into the chilly night, thinking.

YHWH means to claim creation for his own; he means to drive the Elohim from their own story, and none of the others can be moved to oppose him. Only Anat understands the cost of it. Only she sees how the Elohim are needed. Who but she can manifest the blood-hunger that moves the world? Whose voice but hers could carry the cries of war, the call to glory, the savage songs of change? What stupor would consume the lives of men without her? Why will no one fight for her, as she has fought for them?

***

High in a tower sits Moloch, devourer of innocence: Moloch of the seven stomachs; Moloch whose skin glistens with the blood of infants and the tears of their parents; dread Moloch with the body of a man and the terrible head of a bull; Moloch unto whom children are passed through the fire, or used to be, at least; Moloch the abominable, the insatiable. He leans his enormous chest forward, bending at the waist, and he sighs at the pain in his hip, and he pulls great fuzzy slippers onto each of his horrible feet. He sits up, looks at the broken door to his bedroom closet, and sighs again. Creaking at the knees, he stands, walks to his desk, and rummages around, looking for his keys.

The keys are beneath the book he has been reading — *Learn to Code in 30 Days.* Moloch despises this book. It confounds him. He hurls it across the room. The book crashes against the closet door, which falls from its last hinge and collapses against the row of loincloths hung within. On his computer monitor, a conference call is entering its third hour. No one knows that he isn't paying attention: his mic is muted and his camera is off.

Beside the monitor, his phone begins to vibrate.

Anat.

Moloch ignores her call. He picks up the bathrobe hanging over the back of his desk chair, slips it on, and leaves his apartment.

The woman from 34A, the one with the French bulldog, is at the elevator bank. She sees him coming and retreats to her apartment, head down. Moloch, who has never said a word to her besides *hello,* feels an emptiness in each of his seven stomachs. He waits for the elevator to come, aware of the eyes upon him from nearby peepholes. It comes, and he rides down alone, averting his gaze from the reflection in the polished doors.

The lobby is a high-ceilinged white-lit place, with long crystalline chandeliers and walls of shining stone: an ersatz temple. The plastic soles of his slippers make a zip-zip sound on the carpet. The Bald One is here, behind the desk. He does not look upon Moloch. None of them ever do, except for Charles, who works the morning shift. Moloch likes Charles.

At the far end of the lobby is the Bodega™. This is not an actual shop, but an enormous vending machine stocked with snacks, toiletries, cleaning supplies, over-the-counter medications, and other provisions. Between the Bodega™ and the delivery apps on his phone, Moloch has access to almost everything he needs, leaving him more time to devote to his labors. Moloch is working for an internet startup. His boss is 22 years old. Moloch's boss uses expressions like *disruption* and *growth hacker* and *ninja* and *iterate* and *platform agnostic*. Moloch would like to hurl his boss across the room, as he did with the book. He would like to, but he cannot. Moloch works from home.

Indeed, were it not for the meetings of the Elohim, Moloch would never leave his apartment building at all. But he has begun to prefer it this way. He is ill at ease in the world of men.

From the Bodega™ Moloch purchases a packet of Little Debbie brownies and a tube of toothpaste. His enormous fingers tear at the packet as his slippers zip back across the lobby, and he shovels the first of the brownies into his mouth. By the time he reaches his apartment, he has consumed them all.

On his monitor, the call continues. His boss is talking about game changers. Ageless Moloch has lately come to learn new definitions of eternity. He watches his boss for a moment. Some of them whom I have devoured, he thinks, were little younger than you.

He checks his phone: three missed calls; three voicemails. All Anat.

Moloch removes his robe and slippers. He shuffles to the wreckage of his closet door and picks up *Learn to Code in 30 Days.* He puts on his glasses, sits on the bed, and begins to read.

Enki is on his second vodka tonic when Anat calls. He hesitates. It would be hard to hear her, anyway, over the unmelodious wailing from the end of the bar. But it's no use putting her off.

She snaps at him before he can say hello: "Why are you all avoiding me?"

"I answered on the second ring."

"Where are you? What's that noise in the background?"

"I believe it's meant to be Tiny Dancer."

"You're at Winnie's."

"Yes. Why don't you join me?"

Winnie's is a little karaoke joint downtown: once fashionable, then for a time so resolutely unfashionable that it has lately become fashionable again. Mortal fashions, like mortal fates, change so quickly that to Enki's eye they are almost imperceptible. But he is training himself to see them. Here, for instance: a low ceiling; phony wood paneling on the walls and on the front of the long bar; leaded glass lamps hanging like little umbrellas above red vinyl booths; a black-and-red checkered floor; bottles all along the back of the bar, illuminated by the light reflecting from the mirror behind them as well as the light glowing down through faux-stained-glass panels above; a big vase stuffed with wilting chrysanthemums. And of course the laser-disc music machine and the enormous, scratched-up screen on which the lyrics to pop standards scroll over images of young Chinese lovers wandering about in gardens. The appeal of it all, thinks Enki, derives neither from the general nor the specific, but somehow from the interplay of the two. He likes Winnie's for what it is, for its homely dissimilarity to any palace in the sky. But for the mortals around him, he has come to understand, there is an additional appeal to a place like this one: in some sense it relieves the trauma of their passage through time. It suggests that what once was beautiful will one day be beautiful again.

Anat strides in sooner than he was expecting, given how far

away she was when she called. She's wearing dented armor and she reeks of cigarette smoke. The night's chill still clings to her. He recognizes the expression in her eyes: it is the look they take when she has been chasing an enemy who refuses to give her battle.

"Sit," he says. "Dark & Stormy?"

"Always."

Enki waves to Joy Ann, the bartender, who has learned this drink specially for Anat. Joy Ann makes the drink and sets it atop a cocktail napkin. Anat puts the cherry to her amaranthine lips, and she swallows it whole, stem and all.

"Well?" she says.

"Well?" says Enki.

"What's the matter with you? What's the matter with all of you?"

"Nothing's the matter."

"The Enki I know rolls over for no god. The Enki I know doesn't just sit there looking at his hands —"

"I'm still the Enki you know."

"Hardly."

"The difference between us is that I pick my battles. Whereas you pick all of them."

"But this is the only battle. If you don't pick this one, it's over. I can't get my head around all of you sitting there letting him *berate* us like that. Just sitting there like statues."

"Okay," he says, "but I didn't hear you say anything, either."

Anat laughs bitterly. "Well that's just fucking it, isn't it? I *have* been saying something. But none of you will listen."

"I'm not talking about sidebar conversations. I'm specifically saying that you didn't speak up in the meeting. When you had your chance."

"Enki. You've seen what happens when I speak up. I'm answered with eye rolls, if I get any reaction at all."

"Not from me."

"I can see why you're defensive. I don't think any of you *want* me to say anything. Because the truth is you're afraid I'd win the argument. And no one likes a winning goddess. You know what happens to goddesses who win too much? First they fight you. Then they laugh at you. Eventually they just start ignoring you." She stirs her drink, and the rage leaks from her eyes, until only misery remains. "So here we are. Our Götterdämmerung. Our Ragnarök. And I'm the only one who gives a damn, and you all find it embarrassing that I do. You find it funny."

"I don't find it funny."

"You do. I've become a comic fucking figure, because I have the audacity to give a shit. Don't you see what's happening? We are no longer writing destiny. We are *being written*. And the Author has decided to play me for laughs. Pretty soon He's going to cut me out of the story altogether. And then the rest of you. Me first, because no one finds war goddesses believable anymore. But when I'm gone, He'll be coming for the rest of you."

Enki understands that she wants the fight itself as much as she wants the victory. He could argue all night, just to keep her happy. But all the same, she has a point. "You're right," he says. "It's unfair. It's been unfair since long before this business with YHWH —"

"It wasn't always this way —"

"It wasn't. And we're to blame. All of us, not just…Him. Or *him*, lower-case: whatever. You're right. You've been right. We haven't been listening."

"Well, it's too late now."

"Is that what you really believe?"

"It's what you believe, O God of Wisdom. Who am I to second-guess you?"

"A peer. A friend. A goddess. Speak: I'm listening."

Anat signals to Joy Ann, and waits silently for her second drink to arrive. She swallows the cherry, and then she speaks.

The gods gave men life, she says, and it was men who gave the gods their immortality. Each order authored the other, and in so doing, each was author of itself. And from this collaboration sprang the infinitude of stories through which men and gods alike created the universe in all its colors and dimensions, in all its faces and all its manifestations of the divine will; and there is no greater blasphemy, no more monstrous form of oppression, no worse sin against gods or men than to —

"For fuck's sake," she says, interrupting herself. "What is that horrible noise?"

"That," says Enki, "is someone's best attempt at *Tears in Heaven*, by Eric Clapton."

"I don't know how you know so much about this shit."

"I've been trying to learn a little more about the world."

Anat snorts. "My point," she says, "is that we can't let a single voice claim ownership of the whole story."

"It is not the voice that commands the story,'" says Enki, "It is the ear."

"Is that from your guy?"

"Calvino. Yes."

"It sounds suspiciously like an apologetic to me."

"Does it?"

"Have you noticed how his people are always apologizing for him? Why do you think that is? It's because he alone is insufficient to explain the universe."

"I suppose that's true."

Anat leans forward, frowning ferociously, her hand on the lip of the bar. "But don't you think immortality is worth fighting for?"

"I think," says Enki, navigating his words carefully, "that we are perhaps less immortal than we had believed. And the same will go for him, eventually."

"He speaks as if we commit some injustice by growing old."

"He's young. That's how he sees things. That's how we once saw things."

Anat does not reply. She orders another drink.

"Do you want to sing?" asks Enki.

"No," says Anat.

"I'll go up there with you."

"No."

Now there is another voice: a young woman's, singing Cyndi Lauper's *Time After Time*, bringing something from the song Enki has never heard in it before, something at once tremulous and brave. Enki watches her. She glows — only faintly, but it reminds him of the aura about YHWH. Anat, perhaps accidentally, has made the critical distinction: their trouble is not that they are becoming mortal, but that they are growing old. No army, no warrior, no god can fight it.

Anat broods, watchfully, like a general deciding whether to call in her last reserves. Finally he sees a flicker of retreat in her eyes.

"He's going to fuck it up," she says.

"Probably," says Enki.

Anat sighs. She stirs her drink and watches the singer with semi-seeing eyes. When the
song is finished, she turns her gaze back to Enki.

"Tell me," she says, settling back into her seat. "How have you been spending your time? Now that you have decided to spend it."

"Well," says Enki. "I'm seeing someone."

"Who?"

"His name is Todd."

"A man?"

Enki shrugs.

"A mortal," says Anat.

"He's an anesthesiologist."

"Well," says Anat, "we're all mortals now, I suppose."

They drink together, the god of waters and the goddess of blood, and they talk: first haltingly, about the world as it is, and then fluently, about the world as it was. They tell each other stories of the dawn-days, of the immortal deeds by which they made their names.

130

"Remember when you got yourself pregnant?" asks Anat.

"We don't speak of that," says Enki.

"I mean, it worked out okay in the end."

Six drinks into the abyss, Enki at last persuades Anat to join him for a duet. They sing with their eyes locked together, smiling despite themselves, swaying at the hips.

Islands in the stream, they sing, *That is what we are*

To her own surprise, Anat knows all the lyrics.

***

Haddad alone understands: hereafter, they are waiting to die. They busy themselves with charity and sporting pursuits and second careers and eccentric hobbies, but the Elohim are an obsolescent aristocracy, and all it amounts to is killing time. Haddad has little taste for such busywork; he passes his time with long naps and occasional home maintenance. His excursions are limited mainly to the supermarket and the hardware store. And while his closest friends and family still address him as Baal, the honorific has begun to embarrass him. In public, and in his own mind, he is simply Haddad.

But they do not die. Instead, little by little, they fade from view. They who once shone as brightly as the heavenly spheres now stand in line with everyone else: they are turned away at velvet ropes; they scan their own groceries in the self-checkout lane, utterly ignored. "It's nothing like the fate of men," rants Anat. "It's more terrible than that." But Haddad suspects that it is more like the fate of men than men themselves would care to admit.

Some of the gods are bothered by Haddad's fatalism. Anat calls him daily, shouting through the phone about one outrage or another: politics, or the injustices of the academic job market, or the absurd cost of traffic tickets. Enki drops by sometimes for a late-night beer; he asks Haddad probing questions disguised as casual inquiries. Moloch sends Haddad a book: *Learn to Code in 30 Days.* A thoughtful gesture, but the book is unintelligible and anyway Haddad does not need it. He has wealth enough left for a mortal lifetime. Only Shala lets him be. They have always let each other be: it's the secret to their marriage.

Haddad is at his most content in long late-summer afternoons, in bed beside the open window. He lies still, with a half-read book propped open on his chest, listening to the noises of the world: the murmur of wind in the leaves, the hum of traffic on a distant road, the shouts of his children in the yard. And now and then the call of ravens; and now and then the sound, so faint it might only be a memory, of thunder.

Conversations with a Stranger

by E.C. Osondu

He was an older gentleman. He drove an older car, as well. I think the brand has gone out of production. Don't exactly recall the brand name but I think it starts with the letter P. I could tell he was going to love chewing the fat from the way he said my name — not like a question, not in the unsure way most pronounced it but so familiarly and comfortably.

I commented on the car. I complimented him on the fact that it was still running.

"I am going to drive it until the wheels fall off," he said.

"It looks good and clean," I said.

"I can't afford another car. Where am I gonna get the money to pay the car note?"

"Don't these guys have a scheme where they give you a car and you pay over time?"

"Honestly I am too old for all those schemes. Too tired to be under pressure. I am gonna keep flogging this one until it collapses like a horse and dies on me."

We each paused. A brief period of silence. Each alone with his thoughts. Each knowing the silence was not going to last. I was thinking of breaking it when he plunged in and broke it.

"Where are you from?" he asked.

I hesitated for a moment. He read my hesitation as reluctance, even though it wasn't.

"Wait let me guess. I met a guy from your place some time ago. Hold on, it will come to me. Do you speak French?"

"No, I don't speak French."

"You don't speak French?"

"Were you thinking of Haiti?"

"Haiti? No. I know Haiti. They are the *soup joumou* people. I ran around with a bunch of Haitians back in the day. Definitely not Haiti. But never mind, it will come to me. Things take their sweet time to come to you as you get older, but they do come, eventually."

I thought of some smart quip as a riposte, but nothing was coming to me.

"Now it comes," he said.

"It has? That was quick."

"Senegal. Yes, that is the name of the country. Senegal."

I told him I was not from Senegal though Senegal was in West Africa, which happens to be my sub-region so he was not too off the mark.

"Yes, my buddy from Senegal, he's tall and dark skin, you are tall and dark skinned so I make the connection, though he speaks French. Here is the funny thing. He went to the community college; he says he wants to be a Nurse. He did well in all the subjects at the community college. How do you say? He *aced* all the subjects at the community college. All the Math all the Chemistry but he couldn't pass the English. Community College said you must pass English to become a Nurse. So I used to take him to Spanish Action League office for English language conversations. After that he passed the Nursing exams. He's a Nurse now, bought a big white house and car. Now he tells me his wife is going to be a Nurse like him."

I remembered what an immigrant healthcare worker had once told me. He was a Nurse Practitioner and we were talking about healthcare and he said a man with a headache, even if he is a racist is a man with a headache and all he wants is relief — he wants the headache to go away. He doesn't care how thick the accent of his attending physician is, he just wants to get better. Once the headache goes, his racism returns.

I returned to the present.

He was addressing me.

"Look, I shouldn't be driving. Not at my age. See how I drive real slow. When we get on the highway all the other cars are going to be zipping past me. I hold the steering wheel with both hands — *nine and three o'clock style* they call it."

"You are doing fine. I am not in a hurry. I don't like speeding."

"That's nice. Some don't complain but later they rate me shitty and give me two stars."

"You make great conversation, and I am not particularly in a hurry, so no worries," I said.

"Where are you from?" I asked.

"Colombia."

"Ah, Colombia," I said. Three things came to my mind at the mention of the country's name.

"You guys love soccer in Columbia like we do in Nigeria," I said.

"Yeah, some of us do like soccer. Not really for me. Just something on the television while I drink with friends and family," he said.

I laughed. "You guys love Nigerian Highlife music in Colombia," I said.

"*Highlife* music?"

The way he made the word *Highlife* sound so foreign told me it was not something he was familiar with. I decided not to pursue it further.

"I read somewhere that lots of people are moving to Colombia these days. They say it is possible to live cheaply there and the country is beautiful," I said.

"Yeah, Colombia is beautiful but nobody moving there. My friend Mateo traveled back recently, and he ran back here real quick."

"Seriously?"

"Yes, seriously. The cartels and banditos, they control everything", he said.

A pall seemed to wash over us, and we both seemed to observe a moment of silence.

***

"Every day I go to my lawyer about my social security benefit. He keeps telling me he's working on it. Same story everyday nothing changes. I feel too old for this hustle. All the other drivers are young people."

He zagged into this course of the conversation seemingly out of nowhere.

"I thought social security benefits are automatic. If you worked and contributed into it and you are of age, then you should collect."

"Yeah, that's what they say."

"It is the truth," I said.

"Well, you see, I don't got no papers."

For some reason his voice dropped when he said this — like he was whispering some shameful secret to me. I too felt his shame — for about half a minute his shame was my shame.

"When did you come to America?" I asked.

"I came here in the eighties."

"Oh, yeah?"

"Yeah."

"But I heard Reagan granted amnesty to all those who didn't have papers in 1986."

"Yes, he did, I know. Oh, man, I was wild and young. I didn't care about no amnesty. I was doing my thing, to be honest."

"What was your thing?"

"I was getting into trouble. Yes, *trouble* was my thing."

My mind roamed wondering what kind of trouble he meant. Even though American language may not know it, it tended to be more euphemistic than specific on occasion. He cleared his throat and brought me back to the present. We were stuck — the traffic was not moving. He turned off his engine. I wondered if this was a wise thing to do. The car was old — what if the engine didn't start when he wants to start it again? It looked like the kind of car that should have a *check engine* light on, but it didn't and was clean too.

My phone vibrated. A text message came in. It asked if I was safe that they noticed we'd stopped for quite a while now and were wondering if everything was ok. It was from the ride company.

I felt flattered by their solicitousness. It was good to know that a corporate behemoth was carrying out a welfare check on me — how kind and thoughtful.

He was on the phone too. He was explaining to the person at the other end that there was an accident on the highway and that we were fine.

I began to feel important.

Soon a couple of police cars zoomed past. They must have done their work because the traffic began to move again. We drove past the accident scene. One of the cars in the accident had caught on fire and burned to a black and grey husk. Smoke rose from its carcass.

"I am gonna keep fighting until I get my social security payment. This is America," he said.

This is America — a boast that I have heard from different people in the country. I think it probably meant different things to each one but I decided to probe what exact meaning the phrase held for him.

"When you say — *this is America* — what do you mean?" I asked.

"Let me explain. So, I am coming from say Nicaragua, Guatemala, Colombia, doesn't matter. I am coming by foot. You know in this country there are three sets of people — those who come in with their heads, you know those who were born here and there are people like you who come in through the air you fly in like birds and then we who come in by foot."
I said the word *bird* and made flapping gestures. We both laughed. I was going to try to use that to encourage myself in moments of despondency. I must always remember to fly high and soar like the bird on whose wings I came to the country.

"The moment I step foot on American soil after crossing those beautiful rivers you hear about — *Rio Bravo, Rio Grande* and *Rio Whatamacallit.*"

This too made me laugh. He was happy I was laughing out aloud at his jokes.

"As soon as I stepped into American soil," he said, "I heard this voice saying — step this way sir, sir I am talking to you sir, sir, sir…"

"Yes sir," I said.

"Seriously nobody has ever called me sir in my life. I had no idea I was a sir or anything for that matter. I looked over my shoulder to make sure he was not addressing someone else. He was actually talking to me. So that was the first thing America gave to me — a sir."

For me, on the other hand, being addressed as *sir* was something I had never received from a public official out of respect. It was more their way of asserting authority. It was the equivalent of being called — *Mister Man* — in my country of birth. I recalled something someone said about the British — he said once they begin a sentence with the phrase — *I am afraid* — that it simply meant that they had power over you and that they were not afraid of you at all.

"That was the day I knew that this is America. I am gonna keep fighting until they start to pay me that check. Maybe when they start to pay I can even decide to go back to my country and live on a farm and die in peace."

I had not thought of this angle. He could afford a decent quality of life with that social security check if he ever gets it.

"You know the guys from the Islands, you know what they do? When they get their social security check they go back to the Islands, and they live a good life. Let me tell you what other thing they do — they marry a young girl. So, they marry these young girls and they live with the young girl two, three years and boom they fall down dead. Yes they die. Their heart cannot take it anymore."

"You mean they have a heart condition because of their age?"

"No, they die of too much happiness."

I had to laugh at that one. He was pulling my leg, I think. Could it be that he was engaging in what was called *picong* in the Caribbean? But then again, he was not from the Caribbean.

"Don't tell me that when you start collecting that check you are going to marry a younger wife when you return to your country."

"Nah, not me, I don't have the heart for it. I was wild when I was young but not anymore. I just want a simple and quiet life now," he said.

It wasn't the response I was expecting but it was a good response. We were passing an area filled with a certain familiarity for him. There were political billboards with names of politicians that sounded like his own name from both parties. The foods in the restaurants were the kind of foods he knew more than me and the businesses were the typical businesses for such a neighborhood — tax preparation, money transfer, mattress shops and a restaurant named *El Paradise.*

A certain ease came over his mien and he became visibly relaxed and began steering with one hand.

"See my people how they work hard. See this entire neighborhood has come back to life."

Interesting that this environment where he was feeling so much at home was as alien to me as any other place in the country. Even though I passed through it all the time the advertisements for yucca and mattresses, *Ria* and *Monito*, and concerts by some guy who was definitely not Julio Iglesias never felt any less alienating.

I was thinking of something. I was thinking I should not say it. I remembered that this was a country where people pretty much kept their thoughts to themselves except if they worked in television or hosted radio shows — then, in that case — nothing was too ridiculous to say.

I decided to say it to him, anyway. After all, the chances of our meeting again was slim if not non-existent.

"Some people will say that you guys are *taking over*," I said.

"Oh, there's nothing wrong with *taking over*. Everybody takes over sooner or later."

"How so?" I asked.

"When I first came to this country, some other people, your people, used to drive the taxi cabs. Now we have taking over. Why? Because they have moved on to doing something better?"

"Oh yeah?"

"Ok, let me explain. Some people used to be the only ones who could be the President but now look your brother Barack he is the President now. That's what I mean by taking over."

I laughed really hard at that one. Barack, *my brother?*

Before I could pursue that thought any further, we arrived at my destination. I was here for a gathering. I was going to play a game if I ever got bored during the gathering. I would look at each person and try to guess if they had come to this country with their head, their feet or had flown in like a bird.

"Ok, my friend, don't forget to give me a five-star rating," he said.

"You deserve ten stars," I said.

"Five stars is fine. I am not greedy," he said.

I shook his hand, and we parted ways. Like two ships that passed by each other we had peered into the cabin of both our lives and had revealed ourselves to each other. Like the two ships we were confident that the sea called America was so wide that our nautical paths may never cross again. We went our separate ways.

Contributors

Erin Almond grew up in East Hartford, Connecticut and was the lead guitarist for several all-girl metal bands you've never heard of. Her debut novel, *Witches' Dance*, was published by Lanternfish Press in 2019, and her fiction, essays, and reviews have appeared in *The Boston Globe*, *The Sun*, *Colorado Review*, *Literary Mama*, *Normal School*, and WBUR's *Cognoscenti* column. She lives with her husband and three children outside Boston and can be found online at https://erineileenalmond.com.

Susan Buttenwieser is the author of the novel, *Junction of Earth and Sky* (Manilla Press, UK) and the short story collection, *We Were Lucky With the Rain* (Four Way Books. Her writing has been nominated for a Pushcart Prize and appeared in *Pangyrus*, *The Brooklyn Rail*, *City Limits*, *Atticus Review*, *Statorec* and other publications. She has received fiction fellowships from the Virginia Center for the Creative Arts, contributes news features regularly to Women's Media Center and has taught creative writing in New York City public schools, Rikers Island, Bedford Hills Correctional Facility, juvenile detention facilities, homeless shelters and in public libraries.

Paul H. Curtis is a writer and editor living in Yonkers, New York. He is an Associate Fiction Editor, as well as the events coordinator, for *Fatal Flaw* literary magazine in New York. His writing has appeared in publications including *Cherry Tree*, *Levee Magazine*, *The Madison Review*, *Zone 3 Press*, *Inkwell Journal*, *Bridge Eight*, *Prose Online*, and *Rockvale Review*, as well as in *Fatal Flaw*. Find him online at www.paulhcurtis.net or on Instagram @ paul.h.curtis.

Catherine Elcik is a writer, tutor, and writing coach in Winthrop, Massachusetts, who writes fiction about misfits and subcultures. Her short fiction and essays have appeared in *Creative Nonfiction, Brevity,*

Carve Magazine, Narrative, and *The Drum,* among others. She received an Emerging Artist Award from the St. Botolph Club Foundation and a notable essay distinction in The Best American Essays 2022. She holds a BA in Journalism from Northeastern University and an MA in Creative Writing from Boston University. Currently, she's querying agents for her first novel and arm-wrestling with her second. Find her on Twitter and Instagram @ catherineelcik or subscribe to her weekly newsletter for writers at https:// hibou.substack.com/.

Khanh Ha is an award winning author, nine-time Pushcart nominee, finalist for The Ohio State University Fiction Collection Prize, Mary McCarthy Prize, Many Voices Project, Prairie Schooner Book Prize, The University of New Orleans Press Lab Prize, and The Santa Fe Writers Project. He is the recipient of the Sand Hills Prize for Best Fiction, The Robert Watson Literary Prize in Fiction, The Orison Anthology Award for Fiction, The James Knudsen Prize for Fiction, The C&R Press Fiction Prize, The EastOver Fiction Prize, The Blackwater Press Fiction Prize, The Red Hen Press Fiction Award, and The Gival Press Novel Award.

Marie Myung-Ok Lee is the author of the novel *The Evening Hero,* a Good Morning America Book Club Buzz pick. Her journalism and essays have appeared in *The New York Times, The Nation, The Guardian, The Atlantic, The Paris Review* and many others. She is a founder and former board president of the Asian American Writers' Workshop and teaches fiction at Columbia, where she is the Writer in Residence.

E.C. Osondu is the author of two collections of stories *Voice of America* and *Alien Stories* and the novels *This House is Not For Sale* and *When the Sky is Ready the Stars Will Appear.* He is a winner of the Caine Prize, the Pushcart Prize, and the BOA Short Fiction Prize, among other prizes. His fiction has appeared in *The Atlantic Magazine, Harper's, AGNI, n+1, Guernica, Kenyon Review, McSweeney's, Zyzzyva, The Threepenny Review, New Statesman* and many other places and has been translated into over half a dozen languages. A contributing editor at *AGNI*, he has been a Visiting Professor at UT Austin and is currently a professor at Providence College in Rhode Island.

Pamela Painter is the award-winning author of five story collections, and her stories have appeared in numerous journals and anthologies. She has received three Pushcart Prizes and her work has been staged by Word Theatre in London, New York, and LA. Her story, "Doors," is being made into a short film. Her *Pangyrus* story "An Empty Day" is reprinted in *Best Microfiction 2023*.

Ann Russell graduated from Harvard University and holds a PhD in English Literature. After a long career in conservation of art and artifacts on paper, she turned to fiction writing, taking writing classes at GrubStreet in Boston. Her stories have appeared in *Bellevue Literary Review, Epoch, Joyland, Southern Humanities Review, Permafrost*, and other journals. She has been nominated for the Pen/Robert J. Dau Short Story Prize for Emerging Writers. She has been a runner up in contests held by *Greensboro Review, Nimrod, Ruminate*, and *Bellingham Review*.

Joshua Shapiro's fiction has appeared in the *Mississippi Review, Notre Dame Review, Toasted Cheese, Beloit Fiction Journal, Literary Review, G.W. Review, Straylight, Pangyrus, Phoebe*, and *The Main Street Rag*. His short story "Smart Home" won the Mississippi Review 2022 Fiction Prize. He is an alumnus of the Bread Loaf Writers Conference. Read his blog at https://fictionunsafespace.substack.com.